I0763532

Shifter High

SH

PRICKLY TROUBLE

Shifter High

Season 1, Episodes 4 & 5

Written By

A.J. CULEY

Illustrated By

JEANINE HENNING

Cover art and illustrations by Jeanine Henning

Hardback Edition

ISBN: 978-1-7323286-8-6

Edited by J.L. Troughton

A POOF! Press Publication

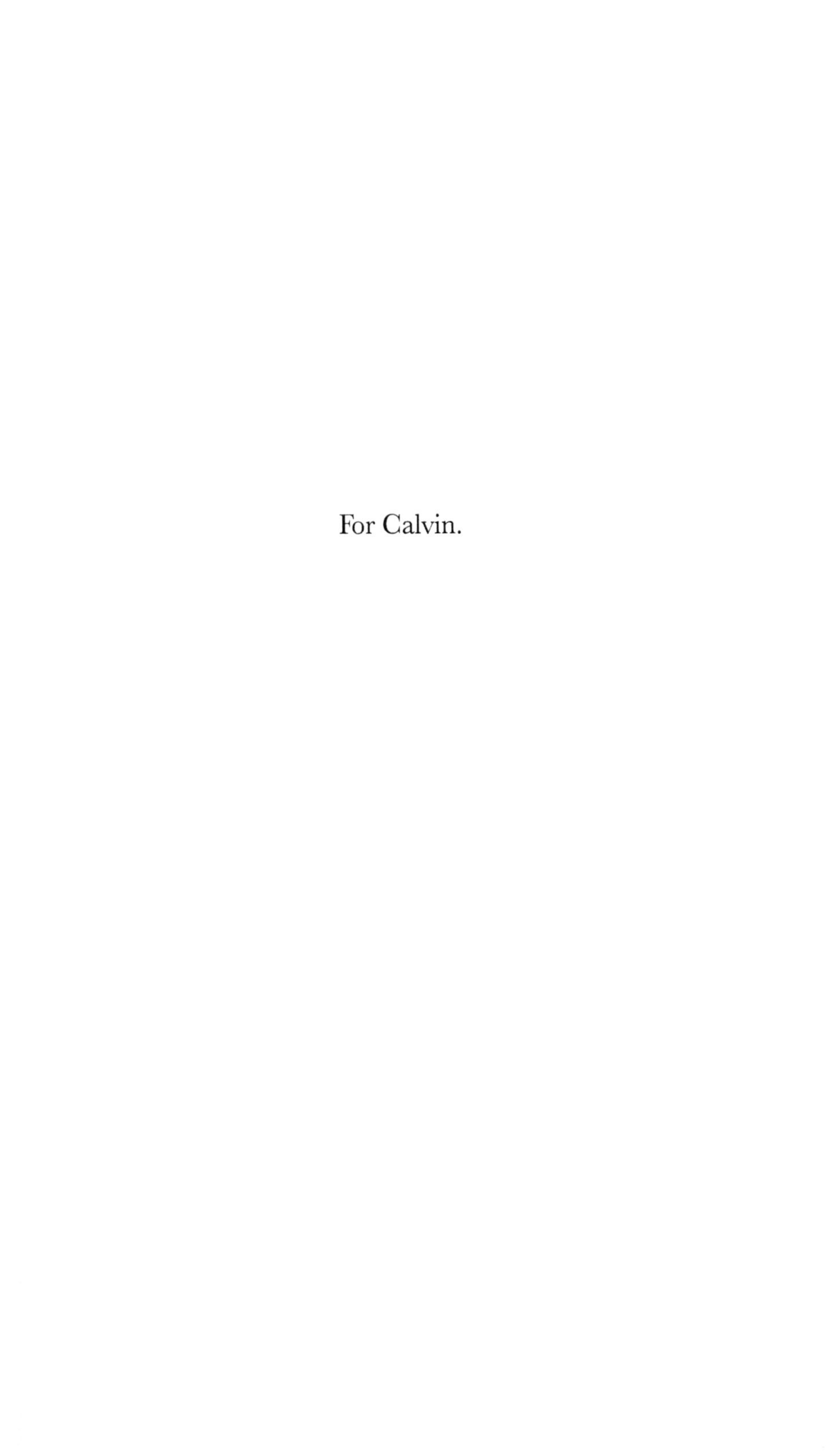

For Calvin.

The Trouble With Quilling (a.k.a. The Spines of Torture)

Shifter High: Season 1, Episode 4

Written By

A.J. CULEY

CONTENTS

"Go away isn't that difficult a concept.
It means GO. AWAY."
- Tessa Hedgehog

"I'm clearly the right shifter for Tessa."
-Alex Hedgehog

"Not even close. Your circling isn't that impressive and your figure eights look more like figure zeros."
- Brock Hedgehog

one

the hedgehog way

AMELIA AND FELICIA walked out of the bowling alley, Felicia's brother, Luis, and her cousin, Sam trailing behind them.

"That was fun!" Felicia bounced at Amelia's side, full of energy as usual. "We should always bowl on Sundays!"

Amelia laughed. "Why Sundays?"

"I don't know." Felicia hopped ahead, then turned to face the boys, all the while still hopping. "What do you guys think? Bowling on Sundays?"

"Sure."

"Definitely."

Amelia laughed. She just didn't get it. She enjoyed bowling, sure, but didn't really understand the enthusiasm all the other kids had for it. It was just bowling, right?

They were coming up to the end of the square, where the four of them would have to split up to head to their respective homes. They paused at the corner.

"Do you want us to walk you home, Amelia?" Felicia asked.

"What? No, of course not. It's in the complete opposite direction from you. I'll be fine."

"I don't know," Sam said. "It'll be dark soon. Maybe we should –"

Amelia rolled her eyes. "I'll be fine, you guys. We should probably get going though."

"Yeah, she's right," Luis said.

"Would you boys just go home?" The voice was snappish and annoyed and the words were so similar to the conversation they'd just been having, it took a second for Amelia to realize it had come from someone not in their group.

"You heard her," another voice said. "Go home, Brock."

"She was talking to you, Alex!"

"Oh, great," Felicia muttered.

Three kids came around the corner. One was Tessa, a girl Amelia recognized from her biology class and from the group of kids who'd brought a scared bunny to her dad's vet clinic the day before. On either side of Tessa were two boys Amelia didn't know.

Tessa didn't acknowledge any of them, just veered off the sidewalk into the street, did a weird zigzagging move past them, then zipped back onto the sidewalk and kept walking.

The two boys did some weird shuffling as they raced after her.

Were they circling her?

Tessa was walking in a strange zigzag formation away from them, occasionally stopping to spin in a circle, then moving forward in a bizarre zigzag pattern again. She occasionally zigged back the way she'd come before zagging forward again.

The two boys, no matter which direction she went, followed her, somehow circling her at the same time, so that they'd be on one side of her one moment, then the other side the next. They never seemed to cross each other's paths, instead keeping pace with Tessa's bizarre movements, all the while arguing with each other, each demanding the other leave Tessa alone.

Amelia just stared. It was the weirdest thing she'd ever seen.

"Holy binkies, those hedge–" Luis stopped in a sudden choking fit.

"Are you okay?" Amelia asked, still staring after Tessa and the two boys. Without even waiting for an answer, she asked, "What's up with those three?"

Felicia laughed. "Oh, nothing. Brock and Alex just like Tessa a lot."

"So they're badgering her?"

"Well…" Sam had a confused look on his face. "I wouldn't exactly call it badgering."

Of course he wouldn't.

"They're just, you know, letting her know they like her," Luis said.

Why were all boys so stupid? "By chasing her? By ignoring her when she asks them to leave her alone?"

Far ahead, Tessa turned away from the two boys circling her and zigged her way back down the sidewalk toward them.

"Look! She's so upset, she keeps changing direction, trying to get them to go away."

"Um, I don't think, I mean–" Felicia wilted under Amelia's glare. "Well, maybe."

"That's what I thought." Amelia turned and stormed toward the two boys. If her friends wouldn't do something to help Tessa, she would.

This was terrible. "What should we do?" Felicia demanded. "Tessa won't appreciate Amelia's interference and those boys have no discretion."

"Come on," Luis said and they hurried after Amelia, arriving just in time to hear her snap at Brock and Alex, "What do you two think you're doing?"

Brock, Alex and Tessa all came to a stop on the sidewalk and stared at Amelia.

Tessa looked about as grouchy as a prickly hedgehog could ever look and Brock and Alex just looked stunned that the human had approached them at all.

"Well?" Amelia demanded.

Brock and Alex looked at each other, then back at Amelia.

"We're showing Tessa our appreciation," Brock said.

Alex nodded.

Amelia glared at the two boys. "By crowding her and harassing her?"

"We're not crowding her, we're circling her," Brock said.

"Exactly! To show our appreciation," Alex said.

Felicia winced and glanced at Luis and Sam. The looks on their faces matched her own. This was not going to end well.

"Well, do it somewhere else!" Amelia snapped. "Tessa already asked you to go home. Ignoring that request is not how you show your appreciation."

The two boys shrugged. "See you tomorrow, Tessa," they said in unison, then turned and hurried away.

Amelia stared after them a moment, probably wondering why they were moving in zigzag patterns. She was so going to figure things out and then they'd all be diggered.

Not that Felicia would really mind. After all, they were friends and it was weird keeping such a huge secret from her friend, but the rest of the town and the Town Council wouldn't see it the same.

The two boys turned a corner and disappeared from sight.

Felicia turned around, Amelia at her side, and that's when she realized Tessa had already walked away. She was pretty far down the sidewalk, moving in her usual zigzag, figure eight pattern, speeding away from them.

Amelia raced after her and with a few sighs and groans, Felicia, Luis and Sam hurried in her wake.

"Are you okay?" Amelia asked.

Felicia wasn't surprised when Tessa just ignored her. Tessa wasn't much for talking or socializing lately.

"I mean really," Amelia said. "They didn't hurt you did they?"

Tessa made a small hedgehog-like grunt, turned and ran up the walk toward her house. At least Felicia thought it was Tessa's house. It could have been her cousin Mary's house.

"Okay, well, nice chatting with you," Amelia called after her.

Once Tessa disappeared inside, Amelia turned and demanded, "Is she always that friendly?"

Felicia giggled. "She's usually pretty nice. You just caught her at a bad time, really."

Amelia nodded. "Yeah, I'd be in a not great mood too if those idiots were hassling me."

"Aw, come on. Brock and Alex aren't that bad," Luis said. "It's just their way."

Felicia winced. Everyone needed to stop talking about The Hedgehog Way before Amelia figured everything out.

"Well, their way is pathetic!" Amelia said. "And you defending them is pathetic too."

"Hey!" Luis looked offended.

"I'm just saying. A girl has the right to say no and if a guy refuses to respect that, he's a pig." Amelia stormed away.

Luis made a huff of exasperation. "Well, yeah." He looked at Felicia and Sam. "I mean, they are hedgehogs."

two

targets

THE NEXT DAY, Amelia couldn't wait for biology. Not because she particularly enjoyed the sciences, but rather because she was anxious to check on Tessa. Unfortunately, biology wasn't until after lunch so all morning long, Amelia looked for Tessa in the hallways, but never saw her.

According to Felicia, Tessa was assigned to Cafeteria A, just like them, but Amelia couldn't find her at lunch either.

"Don't worry," Felicia said. "I'm sure she's fine. And you'll see her next hour, right?"

"I suppose." Amelia wasn't sure why she was so worried about Tessa. There was just something about the way the boys had been circling her that just had all the hair on the nape of her neck standing on end. It was just so… creepy and… weirdly feral.

As soon as the bell rang signaling the end of lunch, Amelia jumped up and raced toward the door. "See you after school!" she called over her shoulder to Felicia and bolted from the cafeteria.

Biology class was around the corner and at the end of a long hallway, so Amelia had to weave her way through a lot of kids to get there. As usual, most of the students moved out of her way, leaving a clear path for her to follow. Occasionally, though, someone popped up to harass her.

"Hey, girl."

Ugh. It was Victor Hyena from calculus and technology.

Amelia kept walking, weaving in and out of the crowds.

"So what? You're too good to talk to me or something?"

Amelia stopped and faced Victor, hands on hips. "Maybe if you didn't sniff my hair, call me prey and harass me all the time, I'd have something of interest to say to you. Right now though, the only thing I have to say is good and bye." She turned to walk away and rolled her eyes when she saw everyone staring at them. "Don't you guys have class or something?" She pushed through a group of teens and kept walking.

It wasn't that she hated her new school. It wasn't even that she disliked the kids. She'd made some really good friends here and even the weird ones, like Victor with his bizarre habits and eyes that shone weirdly when the light hit them just right, weren't really bad. No one had tried to hurt her – not even scary Katrina, who was really intimidating, but now was kind of a friend. They just said things that were so weird and wrong.

Plus it seemed like she was on display half the time. She'd be doing something perfectly normal, like shelling her pistachios at lunch or removing her earrings in class, and suddenly everyone, including the adults, would be staring at her like she'd just done something truly horrifying.

Spotting the biology classroom door ahead, Amelia barreled inside, leaving the chaos of the hallways behind. She absolutely hated walking from class to class. Maybe it was part of always feeling like she was on display, but she felt vulnerable in the halls, like there was a giant target centered on her back.

Stopping a few feet in, she scanned the room and blew out a breath of relief when she saw Tessa seated at the back.

She weaved her way through the desks and plopped down next to her. "Hi!"

Tessa grunted. Which might have intimidated Amelia if she hadn't already been through this with Katrina, whose growl was much scarier than Tessa's. "So, those two boys haven't been bothering you again, have they?"

Before Tessa could answer (or ignore the question since that seemed as likely an occurrence), Alex from the day before plopped into the seat on the other side of her.

"Hey, Tessa," he said.

Amelia stared. "Seriously? Do you seriously have this class with us?"

"I was just going to say the same to you." He looked confused. "I never noticed you in here before."

Amelia didn't even want to know why he'd never noticed the new girl in class. It probably had to do with his obsession with Tessa.

As if the situation weren't bad enough, Brock arrived. "You're in my seat."

Amelia stared at Tessa. "Really? Him too? You have to deal with both these idiots in here?" She glared at Brock. "Too bad. You're not sitting here and harassing Tessa during class. Find another spot."

The low chatter that had filled the room died away and everyone turned to stare at them.

Tessa had a really weird look on her face like she couldn't believe someone had stood up for her. And the rest of the students all looked stunned. What was wrong with these kids? Did none of them get how disgusting this behavior was?

With a huff of exasperation, Brock turned away. "Come on," he said to Alex. "If I can't sit by her, neither can you."

Alex let out a grunt of exasperation, then said, "See you after school, Tessa."

Before she could reply, Amelia said, "Not if she sees you first, you jerk!"

Grumbling under their breath, the two boys went to opposite sides of the room and sat in their chairs sideways, probably so they could still watch Tessa.

Amelia glared at them. "Is it always like that?"

Tessa just stared at her. "How did you do that?"

"Do what?"

"Make them go away. Those two haven't left me alone since school started this year."

"That's ridiculous. Why hasn't anyone done anything? Have you told the teachers?"

Tessa shrugged. "It's just the way it's always been with my kind."

"Your kind?"

Tessa looked away, then said, "Chubby."

Amelia had a feeling that wasn't what Tessa was originally going to say, but she went along with it. "Well, chubby or thin, it's not okay for them to target you. Everyone deserves respect."

Tessa shrugged. "I guess."

"If they won't give you respect, you have to take it."

"How am I supposed to do that?"

"If they keep ignoring your wishes, report them for sexual harassment."

"What's that?"

Amelia was so stunned by the question, she was temporarily

speechless.

Thankfully their teacher called the class to order right then, giving her a brief reprieve.

"I'll explain later," she whispered, even as she wondered how she could possibly unpack such a huge issue like sexual harassment, especially when Tessa didn't even seem to recognize the term. And how was that even possible?

three

bullies

AT THE END of class, Tessa bolted.

"Wait!" Amelia grabbed her books and pushed her way to the door, but by the time she reached the hallway, Tessa was gone.

The rest of the afternoon passed slowly though technology wasn't that bad.

Amelia continued working on her pop culture presentation, which for some reason, was more interesting to her friends, Paulie Porcupine and Katrina Tiger, than their own projects. They kept asking her weird questions like how many zombies she'd actually met and why they liked to eat brains.

Then Victor Hyena leaned forward, sniffed her hair, and wondered out loud if zombies ate the entire head, hair and all, when going for the sweet stuff.

Thankfully the bell rang, preventing Amelia from following through on her instincts, which involved bloody mayhem.

Her final and least favorite class of the day was Calculus.

The only two kids Amelia really knew in that class weren't exactly her friends.

Laney Siamese considered herself to be better than pretty much everyone else and Amelia was no exception. Laney resented that Amelia was seated next to her, forcing them to be partners. Apparently before Amelia's arrival, Laney had been allowed to work independently rather than join a group – big surprise that no one wanted to work with her. As a result, she complained loudly every single class period that she shouldn't have to work with the "outsider." Amelia had been as tolerant as possible, smiling at Laney and basically trying to kill her with kindness, but it just wasn't working.

Every class period, the harassment got worse. And maybe it was because of what Amelia had seen between Tessa and her two little stalkers, but Amelia was pretty much done with bullies.

So when Laney once more, for about the seventy millionth time since Amelia'd enrolled at Shiffer High, complained loudly, "This is the worst pairing in the universe. How can I possibly work under these conditions–" She waved her hand dramatically in Amelia's direction. "–with *that*?" Amelia turned to her and snapped, "Good question, Laney. How can anyone possibly work under these conditions with *your* voice grating in their ears?" She said it in exactly the same tone of voice, with exactly the same inflection that Laney had delivered her complaint.

Dead silence.

"No answer? What a shock." Refusing to look at the other students in the classroom or at Ms. Raccoon, who as usual, was ignoring Laney's drama, Amelia redirected her attention to the calculus problem they'd been working on and solved it without Laney's help.

As usual.

"Well, I never," Laney exclaimed, apparently having finally found her voice.

"Probably not," Amelia muttered. Gathering her courage, she glanced around the room and discovered to her surprise that most of the other students were grinning. And – she peeked at the front of the classroom – so was Ms. Raccoon.

Maybe calculus wasn't so bad after all.

Then Victor Hyena leaned forward and sniffed her hair.

Again.

four

the human way

AFTER SCHOOL, FELICIA hurried to Amelia's locker, dragging Luis, Sam and their friend Mason with her.

She wanted to find out what had happened in biology with Tessa and maybe run interference for her, try to keep Amelia from pestering her too badly.

Tessa was in full-fledged quilling mode, with all her adult spines trying to force their way through the tiny holes left behind by her baby ones. It meant she was a hedgehog on the edge—both itchy and irritable—and Felicia was afraid Amelia might just be the one to push Tessa over it.

"Hi, Amelia!" Felicia hopped over to the bank of lockers, super relieved her friend hadn't left yet.

"Hey, guys." Amelia shoved her bookbag into her locker and grabbed her jacket. "Have you seen Tessa?"

"I'm pretty sure she already left," Felicia said.

"She doesn't stick around after school," Sam said.

"Probably trying to get a head start." Mason chuckled. "Otherwise, she'll have shadows all the way home."

Amelia scowled.

"Mason!" Felicia shoved him.

"What?"

"Don't listen to him," Felicia said. "I'm sure Tessa's fine. Brock and Alex would never hurt her."

"That's not the point." Amelia closed her locker and started walking toward the front doors. "Just because they don't mean anything by it or aren't going to hurt her doesn't make it okay. They're harassing her."

"They're not harassing her," Mason said, "whatever that means. They're just showing her their appreciation."

Felicia, Luis and Sam all groaned.

Amelia came to a dead stop in the hallway. She turned and stared at Mason. "If she doesn't want their appreciation and she asks them to leave her alone and they refuse to do it and continue *appreciating* her—" She made air quotes around appreciating. "—that's harassment!"

"Um, okay, come on." Felicia caught Amelia's arm and pulled her away from Mason, who looked absolutely stunned at her outburst. "Mason didn't mean anything by it. He just doesn't think the way you do."

"That's obvious. You agree with me though, right?"

"Um, well, maybe. I mean, I'm not sure. Yes, I think if she asks them to stop, they should stop, but they're not used to that. It's not their way." Great. Now she was the one talking about The Hedgehog Way.

"Being respectful isn't their way?"

"Um. Well. When you put it like that. I mean–I guess the thing is, they need to be taught a different way, you know? Like no one's ever taught them not to act that way because it's how their dads and uncles and cousins all behave."

Amelia stopped again. "You mean, their fathers courted their mothers this way and it worked for them?"

Felicia nodded. "Pretty much. Yeah."

"Oh, man." Amelia started walking again, leading them out of the school and onto the sidewalk. "What about Tessa's parents?"

"Yeah, probably them too."

Amelia shook her head. "This is way bigger than I thought." She stood there a moment, staring at the sidewalk, hands on hips.

Felicia wanted to ask what she was thinking about, but was honestly afraid to hear the answer.

"Okay," Amelia finally said. "I think I need to go home for this one."

"So you're not going to find Tessa?"

"Yes, but I need to grab a DVD first. I promised Tessa I'd explain what sexual harassment is and I think it'll be easier to just have her watch *9 to 5*."

Felicia had no idea what Amelia was talking about. What was a DVD and how was Tessa going to watch numbers? "I'll come with you!"

"Are you sure? It's kind of a long walk."

"That's okay." Felicia really wanted to know what a DVD was and she didn't trust Tessa not to spontaneously shift into her hedgehog form if Amelia showed up at her house alone.

They started walking.

"Hey. Where're you two going?" Luis asked. "I thought we were going to the ice cream parlor to study."

Amelia made a face (probably because she didn't like most of the flavors there. Who knew humans wouldn't like spinach ice cream?)

Felicia turned to face the boys, but kept hopping backward, keeping pace with Amelia. "We're going to Amelia's house first," she told her brother. "Then we have to find Tessa. Maybe we'll go for ice cream after that."

Luis looked worried. "We should probably leave Tessa alone. I mean, she hasn't exactly been in the best of moods lately."

"Understatement," Mason muttered.

"We're not leaving her alone!" Amelia said. "That poor girl's been harassed by Alex and Brock every single day since the start of school. Of course, she's in a bad mood! No one's helping her, so I'm going to, even if you guys won't."

"Of course we'll help," Felicia exclaimed. She glared at the boys. Why couldn't they just keep their mouths shut? They were riling Amelia up all the more.

Luis rolled his eyes and Sam and Mason looked impatient, but they kept walking with them.

"So, why are we going to your house again, Amelia?" Sam asked.

"To get my DVD. It'll explain sexual harassment way better than I ever could."

"I still don't know what that even means!" Mason said what Felicia was thinking, but would never have said because she had a feeling they'd all know what it was, if they were fully human.

Amelia didn't bother to answer. She just shook her head and kept walking.

Felicia'd never been to a human's house before and the closer they got to Amelia's home, the more curious she became, wondering if The Human Way would be all that different from The Shifter Way. She knew the boys, who had been whisper-debating what sexual harassment might be (their ideas were ridiculous), felt the same way when they all fell silent as Amelia's house came into view.

It was a cute house set at the very edge of Shifterville, built specifically for Amelia and her dad once the town committed to hiring a human for their vet. It was far enough from town and from the shifter housing communities to hopefully keep the humans from stumbling on things they shouldn't.

The outside of the house didn't look much different from a Shifter Home, making Felicia wonder how many (if any) differences they'd find on the inside.

"Come on in," Amelia said as she opened the front door. "Make yourselves at home. I have to check on Squeakers." She hurried down a hall and disappeared.

Felicia wondered what a Squeakers was and why Amelia had to check on it.

"Come on." Sam led them into what appeared to be a living room. "I want to see everything." He didn't say why, but then he didn't have to.

Felicia knew he shared her curiosity about human homes.

Rather disappointing was Felicia's first thought.

The living room had the same type of furniture found in hers: couch, chairs, bookshelves. Nothing too crazy or different.

From the expressions on the boys' faces, they thought the same.

Smelled weird though. Not exactly human. Or not completely human anyway. There were other scents she couldn't quite place. Not human. Not shifter. Something else.

"What's that smell?" Luis asked.

"Smells like Laney, only not," Sam said.

"Don't even say that," Mason groaned. "I do not want to deal with Laney Siamese at all."

Something brushed against Felicia's ankles and suddenly her bunny knew exactly what they were scenting. She let out a shriek and leapt onto the couch.

In the process she dislodged an afghan, revealing—

Felicia shrieked again and climbed over the back of the couch in a desperate bid to escape the three cats curled up on the sofa. Had they been hiding under that blanket? Just hiding there waiting to attack her?

Luis, Sam and Mason cracked up.

"Stop laughing at me!" she wailed. "Cats are scary! They have claws and sharp teeth and they like to eat—" She broke off, not wanting Amelia to hear.

"Eat what?" Luis laughed at her predicament. He was so mean to her!

"Human toes!" she retorted.

Something wet touched Felicia's toe and she froze in terror. "I was only joking," she whispered. She looked down and gulped. One tiny kitten was sniffing her toes while another one was crawling out from under the couch. Felicia's eyes widened as the second kitten inched toward her feet. The first kitten's whiskers tickled her feet.

She was never wearing sandals again!

The second kitten reached her toes, stuck out its tongue and licked them!

Amelia wandered back into the living room. She didn't even look at Felicia or try to help her! Instead, she just walked past the couch and out another door, saying, "I'll be right back. I have to check on Knight." A couple seconds later, she called, "Come here, Knight. Here, boy."

Silence, then they heard what sounded like a gorilla thundering toward them.

A giant dog burst into the living room and Luis, Sam and Mason all gave shouts of pure terror and clambered over the sofa trying to join Felicia.

The two kittens who had settled at Felicia's feet and were diligently licking her toes disappeared back under the sofa. Just in time too because the space behind the couch was suddenly super crowded.

"Ugh, guys. There's not enough room." Felicia tried to push the boys back off the couch, but they were determined. The next thing she knew, Luis, Mason and Sam were all crowded around her, cringing away from the dog who had followed them onto the couch and was now standing on it, head hanging over its back, tail wagging and tongue hanging out.

Amelia appeared in the doorway and stared at the five of them. "What are you guys doing? Knight, get down from there!"

The dog clambered off the sofa and raced across the room to Amelia. He moved super fast for only having three legs!

Amelia dropped to the floor and the dog flung himself into her arms. He climbed all over and around her, wagging his tail and greeting her with huge, slobbery licks of his tongue. Amelia giggled and hugged the dog, calling him "the best, most perfect dog ever."

Felicia just stared. She couldn't believe Amelia wasn't afraid of the dog, especially since she was completely human, with no animal inside to come to her defense.

"Wow," Sam muttered.

"Now I feel like an idiot." Mason climbed back over the couch, carefully avoiding the one cat who was still stretched out there.

The sight of that cat completely unnerved Felicia. Where had the other two gone? Were they waiting to pounce on her again?

While Sam and Luis climbed back over the sofa, Felicia scanned the room, trying to figure out where attack cats might be lurking in wait.

"Come over here, guys," Amelia said. "Come meet Knight!"

Felicia shook her head. "I'll just stay here if that's okay."

At that moment, one of the kittens poked its head out and made a beeline for her toes again.

Amelia left the boys petting the dog (didn't they know dogs liked to eat bunnies?) and walked over to the couch. "What are you doing back there?"

Felicia didn't answer.

Amelia leaned forward and looked down at Felicia's toes, where the second kitten had joined the first.

Amelia giggled. "Oh my gosh, aren't they simply adorable?" She clambered over the sofa, crouched down at Felicia's feet and scooped up both kittens in her hands. She held them close to her face and nuzzled them, just like Felicia liked to do when shifted with her bunny family and friends. "Here!"

To Felicia's horror, Amelia thrust one of the kittens at her and somehow Felicia ended up holding her. She was shocked at how soft her fur was.

"She's a total puffball." Amelia held up the other kitten. "Just like her brother." She cuddled him close to her body.

It was true. Both kittens had long fur that poofed out in all directions. The one Felicia was holding was gray and white while Amelia's was completely black.

After a moment's hesitation, Felicia copied Amelia's movements and brought the kitten close. Thankfully, the kitten's nails weren't very sharp since she began kneading Felicia's shirt almost at once.

After a couple minutes, the kitten stretched out along Felicia's arm and fell asleep, a soft purr rumbling from her chest.

Felicia couldn't believe she'd fallen asleep!

"Not so scary now, is she?" Luis grinned at Felicia while still petting the dog like an idiot.

Felicia didn't answer.

"She needs a good home," Amelia said. "So does her brother. You could adopt them both, one for each of you."

Luis looked horrified. "What do you mean, adopt them? Don't they have parents?"

Amelia shrugged. "Not anymore. My dad rescued them."

Felicia had no idea what that meant. Rescued them from what?

"Why do you have so many animals anyway?" Mason asked.

Felicia could almost hear the words "for a human" floating in the air around him.

Amelia laughed. "Oh, you know. My dad's a vet. He can't just ignore an animal in need, so he keeps bringing them home for us to take care of. Well, at least until we can find another home for them. You've only met a few of his rescues. Most are hiding right now. They're kind of shy around strangers."

Felicia gulped. "H-how many more are there?"

Amelia shrugged. "Not sure. I think we're up to seventeen cats and eight dogs. Or maybe it's nine by now. Plus we have several chinchillas, rabbits and a ferret. Oh! And Squeakers, the guinea pig. My dad's working on the Town Council, trying to convince them to let us host a rescue event."

Felicia had no idea what Amelia was talking about. All she knew was that somewhere in this house were seventeen cats and maybe nine dogs! Sure the kittens were purring puffballs at the moment, but Felicia was now convinced there were fifteen much larger versions of them lying in wait, staring at her, ready to pounce the second she set the kitten down. Not to mention the dogs and ferret!

"Um, so maybe we should go now, yeah?" She was happy to see the three boys had stopped petting the dog and were now standing tensely, looking around, probably afraid eight other dogs were about to pounce.

"Sure. Let me just get Knight settled." Amelia snapped her fingers and the dog followed her out the door.

While she was gone, Felicia and the boys edged their way back toward the front door, trying to keep an eye out for dogs and cats and ferrets that might want to attack.

A moment later, Amelia hurried back into the living room, the black kitten still cradled in her arms. She settled him onto the sofa, turned and noticed Felicia and the boys standing as close to the front door as they could get without actually leaving the house.

She raised an eyebrow and walked over to them. "Were you planning to keep Ms. Poof?"

"What?"

"I mean, she obviously loves you, but I think if you're going to take her, Luis should take Mr. Floof so she doesn't get lonely. What do you think?"

"Oh!" Felicia gasped. "Oh, no. Our parents wouldn't– I don't think. Here." She held the gray and white kitten out to Amelia, who carried her back to the sofa and settled her next to her brother.

"All right then!" Amelia hurried to them, then stopped. "Oh, wait!" She turned and raced across the room to the big cabinet that stood against one wall. She flung open the doors, dropped to her knees and pulled out a stack of narrow books and started to flip through them.

"What's that?" Sam breathed, stepping forward.

Amelia glanced over her shoulder at him. "What's what?"

"That!" He pointed to the giant black box that filled most of the space behind the cabinet doors.

Amelia looked up at the box, then slowly swiveled to face him. "You mean the TV?"

Felicia dug her elbow into Sam's side. It was obvious just from Amelia's response they should know what a TV was.

"Um, no. I thought I saw a spider."

It was a completely ridiculous excuse, but Amelia just rolled her eyes, turned back and continued going through stacks of books, muttering to herself.

A couple minutes later, Amelia leapt to her feet, exclaiming, "Found it!" She shoved the stacks of books back into the cabinet, closed its doors and hurried toward them.

"Found what?" Mason asked.

"*9 to 5*!" She exclaimed, waving the book at them, only it wasn't really a book at all. It was shaped like one, but it had no pages. "Come on. Let's get Tessa!"

"Great," Luis muttered as they hurried after Amelia. "Prepare to get mauled by one very prickly hedgehog."

five

popped corn

AMELIA KNOCKED ON Tessa's door, then glanced over her shoulder at her friends.

They were all acting super weird today. Well, honestly, they acted weird every day. But today seemed to the extreme. Instead of joining her on the porch, they were hanging out on the front lawn, looking uncertain.

Luis looked especially nervous, as if he might break into a run at any minute.

Before she could ask if he was all right, the sound of the door opening had her turning back to face it. "Tessa, hi!"

Tessa grunted.

"Here! I brought you something." Amelia handed her the DVD.

Tessa stared down at it. For a moment, Amelia thought she wasn't going to say anything, but then she asked, "What is it?"

"It's a movie about sexual harassment. I thought maybe it'd be easier for you to watch this than for me to try to explain it."

"Ooh, a movie?" Felicia exclaimed, suddenly appearing at Amelia's side in a series of excited hops. "Are we going to the movie theater to watch it?"

"Oh. Well. No. I mean, it's a DVD. I thought Tessa could watch it on her DVD player."

Everyone stared at Amelia.

"Or, I mean... do you have a DVD player?" she asked Tessa.

Tessa shook her head silently.

"Oh. I hadn't really thought. I guess that makes sense. Everyone's streaming everything these days. Well, I guess you guys could come to my house and we could watch it–"

"No, no, no, no!" Sam, Mason, Luis and Felicia all shouted at the same time, making Amelia and Tessa jump in fright.

Tessa let out a hissing sound, stepped back and slammed the door in Amelia's face.

Amelia huffed and glared at Felicia and the boys, hands on hips. "What the helvetica?" Without waiting for an answer, she turned and knocked on Tessa's door again. "Tessa, come on, open the door. Please. They didn't mean to startle you."

The door slowly opened again and Tessa stood there looking annoyed.

"So, do you want to go to–"

"The movie theater and watch the movie with us?" Felicia shouted, once more making Amelia jump.

"Holy nibbles and bits, Felicia! Tone it down already. And I'm pretty sure the theater isn't going to let us play some random DVD. We'll probably have to watch whatever lame movie they have playing and–"

"Okay!" Felicia hooked an arm through Tessa's and pulled her onto the porch. "Let's go to the movies!"

Tessa rolled her eyes, but didn't protest. Instead she turned and shouted into the house, "Going out, Ma!"

Felicia dragged her down the steps, calling back to Amelia, "Close the door, will you?"

Amelia huffed, closed the door and hurried after her friends. "But I wanted Tessa to watch *9 to 5*!"

Felicia just waved an arm and kept walking.

It was almost as if she didn't want to go back to Amelia's house.

Amelia thought about that for a minute, remembering how Felicia had been standing behind the couch when Amelia returned to the living room. The more she thought about it, the more she wondered. Had Felicia been playing with the kittens or had she been hiding from them?

And then it dawned on Amelia.

Felicia was afraid of cats!

Which was kind of strange given their town functioned as an animal sanctuary. You'd think Felicia would be used to all kinds of animals and not be freaked out by a couple house cats.

Amelia vowed to drag Felicia home with her as often as possible over the next few weeks. She'd have Felicia turned into a bonafide cat lover in no time.

But first, she had to help Tessa with her problem.

By the time they reached the town square, their group of six had grown to eleven. Amelia wasn't sure where all the kids had come from, but it seemed everyone wanted to join them at the movies. She had no idea why.

The theater hadn't changed its one movie listing since Amelia'd arrived in town and that one movie had been made long before Amelia's birth. Surely everyone had already seen it and that was why the theater always looked deserted.

"Are we sure the theater's even open?" she asked.

"Of course it is!" Katrina Tiger said as she pushed her way to Amelia's side and slung an arm around her shoulders. "It's about time you took us to the movies!"

Amelia wanted to ask why it was up to her for the entire town to go to the movies, but she wasn't sure she was ready for the answer, so she didn't say anything at all. If the theater was anything like the bowling alley, Amelia wasn't certain they'd be watching any movies tonight. She certainly didn't know how to run a movie theater.

When they finally reached the town square, Amelia was horrified to see an even larger group of teens waiting for them on the sidewalk under the giant marquee that read, "Jack Nicholson in The Shining."

Felicia giggled when she saw the crowd. "I guess everyone had the same idea."

"Or someone told them we were going to the movies," Katrina said dryly.

That sounded about right. Amelia had noticed the boys were on their phones a lot as they walked toward town. Probably texting everyone they knew. Just great.

"What movie are we going to see?" A girl Amelia recognized from her English class asked excitedly.

"Amelia brought a V-D… V… D," Felicia said, sounding very much like she had no idea what that was.

Amelia sighed and pushed her way through the crowds toward the front door. "It probably won't work. It's not like movie theaters have DVD players, so we'll probably end up having to watch *The Shining.*" She shuddered at the thought. The twins were just freaky and Jack Nicholson always gave her chills.

She pulled on the door, half expecting it to be locked, but not really surprised when it swung open. "It's so dark in here. I have no idea where the lights are."

"I'll get them," Katrina pushed passed and walked into the dark theater. A few minutes later, lights started coming on.

"Oooh! Corn!" A boy Amelia didn't know raced past to the candy counter. He leaped over the counter, grabbed a bag by the popcorn display and started filling it with kernels of corn from the jar standing there.

Amelia shuddered and hurried over. "You're not supposed to eat it like that."

He froze, one hand halfway to his mouth. "I'm not?" He looked super disappointed.

Why were these kids so weird when it came to food? "You're supposed to pop it."

He looked horrified. "Pop it? But I don't want to eat crumbs. I like the crunch."

"Not that way. Here." Amelia grabbed the bag from him and dumped the corn back into the jar and then studied the popper. It looked kind of complicated.

She opened the doors below it and was super relieved to see an instruction manual lying next to a bunch of paper bags. She grabbed the manual, closed the door and stood up.

She found the light and power switches and turned them on. She checked the manual again and said, "Okay, we have to let it warm up for five minutes."

She turned and discovered the entire lobby was full of teens staring at her intently.

"What's that thing gonna do to my corn?" The boy beside Amelia asked.

"Pop it. Trust me, you'll like it."

He looked doubtful, but nodded.

"What's your name anyway?"

"Devon Raccoon."

"Nice to meet you, Devon. I'm Amelia."

He nodded.

Amelia looked over at Felicia. "So is this like the bowling alley? No need to pay for snacks or whatever?"

Felicia nodded. "The Town Council will replace anything we use."

"Okay, well, while we're waiting for the popper to warm up, does anyone want a drink or some other kinds of snacks?"

Felicia joined Amelia behind the counter and they began handing out concessions.

Felicia kept sending kids to Amelia to answer all kinds of weird questions. Like what a candy bar was. When Amelia said it was made of chocolate and nuts, about half the kids got excited while the other half looked really sick.

"Why would they ruin a perfectly good nut by adding chocolate to it?" one kid muttered.

"I want to know why someone would add nuts to a perfectly beautiful bar of chocolate." Another kid retorted.

Amelia rolled her eyes. "There are bags of peanuts over there." She pointed to some hanging at the other end of the counter. "And these chocolates have no nuts." She held up a bag.

The kid complaining about the nuts grabbed the bag and stared at it. "Kisses. That's a really weird name." He shrugged and wandered off.

Amelia went back to the popper and measured out some corn and oil and added them to the pan at the top. She then shook in some salt, closed the pan and the doors, then stood by and waited. A loud pop sounded.

Everyone but Amelia jumped.

She glanced around.

The hum of noise in the room died down as everyone turned to stare at her and the popper.

Another pop sounded and everyone jumped again.

Amelia couldn't believe they'd never had popcorn before. She shook her head and turned back to the popper. It took a few minutes, but eventually the popping was over. She opened the doors, turned the handle and dumped the popcorn into the basin.

She quickly scooped some into a bag and handed it to Devon, who stared at it suspiciously.

Amelia turned back to the popper and added more kernels, oil and salt to the pan. She closed everything and eyed the amount of popcorn that was left in the basin. She then glanced around the room at the many teens crowded in the lobby and sighed. This was going to take a while.

"Well, Devon?" One kid called. "Try it!"

Devon was holding a piece of popcorn between his fingers, still staring at it. "How did you make it do that?"

"Do what?"

"It used to be hard. Now it's all fluffy."

"Heat and oil. That's pretty much all it took."

He lifted the kernel, took a deep breath and popped it into his mouth. His eyes got wide as he chewed and swallowed.

"Well?" Jake Tiger demanded.

Devon didn't answer, just fished out another piece and ate it too. He ate a couple more before finally announcing, "Weird. Completely different. But not bad." He poured a handful into his hand and wandered through the room offering everyone a "popped corn sample."

Over the next hour, Amelia worked the popper and handed out bags, including three more to Devon, who decided that popping was the best thing ever done to corn.

Tessa and Luis had joined her behind the counter and were operating their own popcorn machines.

Amelia had seen Brock and Alex in the crowd, so she was pretty sure Tessa was popping corn to escape them, but no matter what the reason, Amelia was grateful for the help.

The crowd slowly dwindled as people got their popcorn and wandered into the theater.

Deciding it was time to go set up the movie, Amelia grabbed Tessa, turned their poppers over to Sam and Mason, and went off to find the projection booth.

She was terrified to see it. What if it was an old fashioned booth where she'd have to figure out a movie reel? Or what if it was a new digital booth with all kinds of complicated equipment? No matter what it looked like, Amelia figured she'd need hours, if not days, to figure it out. She might have some technical skills, but she'd never worked in a movie theater before.

There had to be fifty kids in the theater right now, expecting her to show them something amazing and her choices were *9 to 5* or *The Shining* on equipment she'd never used before.

By the time they found the projection booth (it was in an upstairs hallway), she was pretty panicked.

The moment they stepped into the room though, all the panic disappeared.

Everything downstairs had looked so authentically like a real movie theater, she'd expected something horribly complicated upstairs. Instead, it looked like something she might find in her own living room mixed with some familiar classroom equipment. There was a projector mounted on the wall, pointed out a window to what Amelia assumed would be the movie screen. The projector was connected to some equipment on a table.

Felicia and Tessa hurried over to a window in the wall and exclaimed over their view of the theater below.

"Look! There's Jake and Katrina," Felicia said excitedly.

Tessa sighed. "And Alex and Brock."

Amelia walked over to the table and picked up a remote. She pointed it to the projector and pushed the power button. She then examined the equipment, which was just a receiver and a DVD player. She turned them both on, then asked Tessa for the DVD.

Silence.

Amelia looked at Tessa, who shrugged. "You brought it with you, didn't you?"

Tessa nodded, but raised her hands to show she didn't have it now.

"Did you set it down somewhere?"

Tessa shrugged again.

Amelia sighed. "I bet it's behind the counter somewhere. I'll go find it."

She'd just reached the door when a cheer rang out from the theater below.

"It's playing! The movie's playing." Felicia hopped up and down excitedly, staring down at the movie screen.

"What movie?" Amelia asked suspiciously.

"The Shining." Felicia turned to Amelia, a bright smile on her face. "Come on! Let's go watch it!" She hooked her arms through Tessa's and Amelia's and pulled them both out of the booth, down the stairs and into the theater, where huge vistas of mountains and a small car driving along a lonely road filled the screen.

Amelia shuddered. This was not the movie she would have ever chosen to sit through again. Maybe she could sneak out in a little bit and swap DVDs.

"This way!" Felicia led them down a row, pushing past several other teens to plop down on an empty seat in the middle of the row.

Amelia sat beside her and Tessa sat on Amelia's other side.

A couple seconds later, Felicia leaned over and whispered, "The music's creepy."

"I know," Amelia whispered back. "Maybe I should go switch DVDs."

"No way!" Felicia said. "This is going to be great."

It wasn't great at all.

Every time Jack Nicholson dropped an F-bomb, Amelia cringed, worried they were going to get in trouble for watching what she was now sure was an R-rated movie.

Plus it was terrifying!

It wasn't long before all three of them were slouched in their seats, watching the movie through their fingers.

"This is awful," Felicia whimpered. "Awful."

And then it got worse.

"Shit," Amelia hissed. "I completely forgot there was nudity in this. Are we going to get in trouble for watching it?"

Felicia stared at her. "Why?"

Amelia didn't know what to say so she just shrugged.

"Who cares about nudity?" Tessa whispered. "I'm freaked out about the creepy little girls."

Then both Felicia and Tessa let out a scream (along with a lot of other people in the theater) and dove for the floor.

Amelia couldn't take her eyes from the screen.

"Tell me when it's over," Felicia whimpered.

Amelia couldn't answer. She couldn't even breathe.

Tessa and Felicia slowly climbed back into their chairs to continue watching.

"Can I please switch the DVDs now?" Amelia whispered to Felicia.

"No!" Both Tessa and Felicia exclaimed, eyes riveted to the screen once more.

By the time the film was over, Amelia felt as if she'd been put through the ringer. Somehow this viewing was so much worse than when she'd watched it in her living room with a couple friends two years before.

The fear in the theater was palpable.

She'd never felt anything like it and she'd been to a number of horror films through the years.

This audience was so riveted, it was almost as if they became part of the movie. Every scream and plea by Shelley Duvall, every crazy look on Jack Nicholson's face, every nightmare vision Danny Lloyd had sent ripples of horror through the audience.

By the end of the movie, Amelia could hardly stand, her legs were shaking so badly.

Felicia and Tessa each clutched an arm as they walked out of the theater into the bright lobby.

"That was the worst thing I've ever seen," Tessa said.

"We weren't supposed to watch that anyway. I wanted you to see *9 to 5.*" Amelia hurried behind the counter to where Tessa had been popping popcorn. The DVD was lying on the counter to the left of the popper. "Thank goodness." She grabbed it and rejoined her friends.

"I never-never-never saw any-anything like that, Amelia-Melia," Paulie exclaimed as he raced over to them. "Melvin-Elvin said it was the most horrify-horrifying thing he'd ever seen! We can't wait to see another-other one."

"Melvin's here?" Amelia looked around. "Where is he? I didn't see him in the theater."

"We were up-up-up in the balcony. He had to run-run as soon as the movie let out, let out, but he said to tell you thanks-thanks. Gotta go-go-go. See you guys later-later!" He ran out.

"That movie was terrifying," Laney Siamese snapped as she stormed up to them. "I can't believe you dragged us here to watch something so awful, Amelia Finch!"

Amelia rolled her eyes, but before she could say anything, Katrina, who had been walking by at just the right moment, stopped and said, "Awful? Don't be ridiculous, Laney. That movie was amazing! I had no idea hum–um." She coughed and then continued, "I had no idea movies could be so interesting. You have more, right, Amelia?"

"Um, yeah, sure. They're at home though. Except for *9 to 5*."

"Well, it's too late to watch another one tonight," Felicia said. "Maybe tomorrow after school?"

"Sure." Amelia said.

"Cool." Katrina walked away again.

Amelia turned to Tessa. "I'm really sorry. I know I promised to show a movie that would explain sexual harassment, but–"

"It's okay." Tessa smiled. It was the first smile Amelia'd ever seen on her face. "I had fun."

"Really? I thought you hated the movie."

"No. It was great!" Tessa exclaimed. "I mean I feel so much better now. I don't know why, but it's like that movie just got rid of all my tension."

"Yeah," Amelia said. "It's the adrenaline rush. You're probably experiencing the crash."

"Well whatever. It was amazing. And I'm totally up for another crash tomorrow night."

"Me too!" Felicia agreed.

Amelia laughed. "Sounds good."

"Hey, Tessa!" Brock suddenly appeared in front of them, Alex at his side. "We looked for you inside, but couldn't find you."

"Yeah, you should have waited for us," Alex said. "We would have sat beside you, comforted you during the scary parts."

Amelia groaned.

Tessa stiffened and began to scratch her arms, where a couple bandages were.

"She didn't need your comfort," Amelia told them.

"Yeah," Felicia said. "You two should go home."

Both boys scowled.

"Are you sure, Tessa?" Brock asked.

"We're happy to walk you home," Alex said.

Tessa shook her head and scratched at her elbow.

Amelia sighed. "Just go."

"Okay. See you tomorrow, Tessa." Brock walked away.

"Bye, Tessa." Alex followed him.

"Come on," Amelia said. "Let's head out."

As they walked out of the theater, Amelia caught bits and pieces of conversations. Everyone was raving about the movie. Even the kids who seemed to hate it couldn't wait to hate another one. She grinned and shook her head. She really didn't understand her friends, but they sure made everything a lot of fun.

six

six thousand spines

THE NEXT DAY in technology, Amelia looked up copyright issues. It had occurred to her that maybe showing DVDs at a movie theater wasn't exactly legal. Turned out she was right.

Maybe *The Shining*, since it was purchased for the theater itself, had been okay to show. Maybe the Town Council had purchased licensing rights for it, but she sure didn't have them for *9 to 5*.

The question was did she care? There was this whole thing about how if a movie was used for educational purposes, it wasn't copyright infringement, but since it was going to be shown in a public movie theater, and she wasn't exactly a teacher or planning to give a lecture in conjunction with the movie, it probably wouldn't qualify for that exception anyway.

The whole issue made her head hurt and she finally decided she just didn't care.

Maybe it wasn't the right thing to do, but sharing her movies with the town was for the better good. Maybe they'd learn something, like what sexual harassment was, and gain an appreciation for the arts.

So after school, she led an even larger group to the theater where she taught more students how to run the poppers, set up different kids handing out snacks and drinks and showed Felicia and Tessa how to switch out the movies in the booth.

"Okay, Melvin-Elvin. Coast is clear." Paulie beckoned Melvin into the theater.

The lobby was deserted and the doors to the movie room were closed.

"Come on." Paulie led the way up the stairs to the door at the back of the balcony. "Jake said he'd hold seats for us again. Ready?" He waited until Melvin nodded before opening the door.

Melvin held his breath a moment, then inhaled slowly. A mix of scents rushed in. Tigers, wolves, hedgehogs, rabbits, porcupine (the last was Paulie). He waited. Nothing happened so he slowly stepped into the darkened theater.

Paulie waved him over to where Jake had saved them seats.

Melvin made his way down the aisle and then disaster struck.

"Melvin Moose, sit down!" Laney Siamese leaned forward to whisper-shout at him and a heady rush of girl-cat scent broke over him in a wild wave.

Melvin's antlers exploded from his head in a burst of motion, almost toppling him to the floor.

He froze, afraid to move for fear of knocking someone out with his antlers. Hey, it had happened before. And more than once.

"Oh my gosh, sit down, sit down, sit down, Melvin-Elvin!" Paulie rushed him, grabbed his arm and pulled him down into a seat.

"Really? When are you going to learn to control your rack, Melvin Moose?" Laney slapped the back of his head. "How are we supposed to see through your antlers? You need to change spots with us right now!"

There was a scramble of movement as the girls in the back row climbed over the seats in front of them and settled all around Melvin, who was still frozen in place, afraid to move in case he speared one of them with his tines.

"Go on!" Laney shoved his arm. "Go back there. To the back row where your rack isn't obstructing our view."

Melvin sighed and slowly lumbered to his feet, which wasn't as easy as it looked, given the giant rack on his head.

Paulie and Jake climbed over the seats, then each leaned over and grasped one of Melvin's arms. They helped pull him up into the back row, all while carefully avoiding his antlers.

Other than a couple minutes at the start of the movie when a weird shadow floated at the bottom of the screen, almost as if someone was making finger shapes of antlers in front of the projector, things went really well.

9 to 5 was an entirely different movie from *The Shining*, but it was just as riveting, and at least for Amelia, was a lot more fun. She enjoyed listening to her friends laugh at the antics of the women on screen and was also gratified to hear sounds of outrage whenever Mr. Hart harassed the women.

When the movie was over, Tessa didn't move. Instead she turned to Amelia and said, "I don't understand. I mean, Brock and Alex aren't my bosses, so how is what they're doing sexual harassment?"

Amelia sighed. "It's the same thing, just a different setting. Mr. Hart chases the women around his desk at work. Brock and Alex chase you everywhere."

"Hold up." Katrina leaned forward from where she was sitting in the row behind them. "What are you guys talking about?"

Amelia explained how Brock and Alex had been acting and Katrina scowled. "How long has this been going on, Tessa?"

Tessa shrugged. "I don't know."

"A week? A month?" Katrina asked.

"Well, I mean. Longer than that."

"How much longer?" Katrina looked furious.

"Since last summer I guess."

"That long?" Felicia asked. "Why didn't you say something, Tessa?"

Tessa shrugged. "They don't mean anything by it. They're not bad guys."

"Maybe not," Amelia said, "but you have a right to not be harassed every time you leave your house."

"Wait. This is happening every time you go out, Tessa?" Katrina looked stunned.

"Well, not every time."

Amelia just stared at her.

Tessa flushed. "Okay. Well. Most days, yeah."

"That is so not okay," Katrina said. "You want me to deal with them? Just say the word. I'll make them stop."

Amelia's eyes widened. She had no idea what Katrina planned, but she just knew it wouldn't be pretty.

"Oh, no." Tessa shook her head emphatically. "I'm sure it'll be fine."

"And if they don't listen when you ask them to back off, what are you going to do?" Amelia asked.

Tessa shrugged again.

"You've gotta report them, Tessa. For sexual harassment. All right?"

Tessa nodded.

"Hey what's taking you guys so long?" Luis called from the back of the theater. "Most everyone's left already. You coming?"

The girls stood and filed out. When they reached the main aisle, Katrina slung an arm around Tessa's shoulders. "Come on, hon. I'll walk you home. No one's gonna harass you as long as I'm around."

Tessa threw a slightly panicked look over her shoulder at Amelia.

Amelia shrugged and gave her a little wave. Tessa's house wasn't exactly on Amelia's way home, so she was grateful Katrina was taking Tessa under her wing. Surely Alex and Brock wouldn't be stupid enough to harass her now.

Tessa's hedgehog was not thrilled to have a tiger walking them home. In fact, the further away from the theater they walked, the more stressed out her hedgehog became. She could feel her skin tightening, all those spines beneath the surface scratching at her insides, making everything itch.

She desperately wanted to curl into a ball, but she battled back the urge. She had to get home first.

"Hey, Tessa!"

"Hi, Tessa!"

Brock and Alex popped out from behind a bush to stand in the middle of the sidewalk.

"We'll walk her the rest of the way," Brock told Katrina, reaching for one of Tessa's arms.

Katrina snarled and stepped in front of Tessa, blocking his reach. "Did you ask them to walk you home, Tessa?"

Tessa could barely force the word out, so frantic was her hedgehog at this turn of events. "No."

"Do you *want* them to walk you home?"

"No." This time the word came a little easier.

"You heard her," Katrina said. "Go home and leave her alone."

Tessa's hedgehog eased off a little as it accepted that Katrina was trying to protect them.

"You just don't understand," Brock said. "This is how we do things."

"Yeah," Alex said. "She's a hedgehog. We're hedgehogs. She has to choose."

"Choose what?" Katrina sounded incredulous.

"One of us," Brock said.

"Are you serious? Tessa doesn't have to choose anyone until she's ready and if she's never ready, then she doesn't ever have to choose. That's the way it works in the 21st century. Now go home."

"But that's not the way it is for hedgehogs," Alex said.

Katrina turned and stared at Tessa. "Is he serious?"

Tessa nodded. Hedgehogs took their mating rituals very seriously.

Katrina's eyes went feral and her skin was suddenly banded in stripes of orange and black. She whirled on the boys and snarled, "Leave Tessa alone or my tiger will have itself a hedgie snack."

The boys' eyes widened and they both began to back away.

"Yeah, okay, sorry. See you later, Tessa," Brock said.

"Later," Alex said.

They turned and hurried across the street where they disappeared into the shadows and scurried away.

Tessa released the breath she'd been holding and watched as Katrina paced and battled back her tiger.

A sharp stabbing pain exploded from one of Tessa's arms and a spine popped free. "Ouch," she muttered and carefully grasped the spine and pulled it loose. A tiny bead of blood appeared where the spine had been.

"That looks painful," Katrina said. "How do you stand it?"

Tessa shrugged. "It's not that bad. I figure about a thousand of my adult spines have already come in."

"Out of how many?"

"Six thousand or so."

"Holy hacking furballs. I would have killed someone by now. Probably those idiots. I mean, here you are with quills–"

"Spines," Tessa corrected.

"Spines popping through your skin on a regular basis and those idiots keep following you. I'd have bitten their heads off by now."

"Easier to ignore them. And hide."

"Oh, no. You're a shifter, even if you are little. We don't hide and we don't take scat from anybody."

Katrina's words came back to Tessa as she hurried to class the next day.

She absolutely hated P.E.

Everything about it made her anxious, beginning with just the process of getting there on time.

She ran as quickly as she could, but her short legs just couldn't manage the figure eights as quickly as other shifters might. Not that other shifters ran in figure eights. It was just something peculiar to her kind, this compulsion to never run in a straight line. It usually took twenty-seven figure eights to make it all the way to P.E. from English class, though sometimes it took twenty-nine if the hallways were unusually crowded.

"Hey, Tessa!"

"Hi, Tessa!"

She hurried faster. A quick turn and then another – that made twenty-three figure eights. Only four more to go.

"I'll walk to you to P.E., Tessa," Alex said as he circled her.

"It's my turn!" Brock began circling as well, though he was going the opposite way.

Tessa ignored them both and raced through numbers twenty-four and twenty-five.

Alex and Brock continued their circling, which interfered with her figure eight-making, causing her to have to turn when she didn't want to turn and stop when she wasn't ready to stop.

Brock snorted at Alex who puffed his displeasure in response. Brock hissed and turned on his heels to follow Alex in his circling.

Great. Any moment they were going to butt heads again.

Tessa could feel the spines on her head peeling away from her scalp, standing straight on end. Of course, they took most of her hair with them, so that was just great. She'd now have to spend the entirety of P.E. with her hair sticking out in all directions.

It usually took a lot longer and a lot more stress to make her spines stand up like this, but the quilling process was accelerating, her hedgehog was pricklier than ever and these two idiots were driving her mad.

She was almost there now, racing through the final figure eight.

Alex got in the way of her final turn, though, circling her with Brock on his heels, and remembering Katrina's statement that shifters don't take scat from anyone, Tessa lost her temper.

Swinging toward them both, she hissed and clicked her annoyance.

They froze and stared at her, probably surprised her hedgie was so close to the surface.

Three more spines popped up on her head, and then, in a series of sharp needle-like stabs of pain, spines burst free from her face – three at once, dotting her cheek, chin and forehead – then from her shoulders, arms and five at once on her feet.

The pain was so sharp and intense, Tessa hissed again. Reaching up, she pulled free the spine from her chin and contemplated stabbing the boys with it. She looked up at them and could feel her pupils expanding. Her hedgehog was very close.

Alex's eyes widened, which had to mean her hair and spines and eyes were *insane*. "Um. Okay, well, I guess we'll see you inside, Tessa."

"Yeah. Inside." Brock grabbed Alex's arm and pulled him away from Tessa, toward the boys' locker room.

With a final hiss and two clicks for emphasis, Tessa turned and swung through the final curve, sliding into the gymnasium just as the bell rang.

She stalked across the gym toward the girls' locker room, ignoring the way the other kids' eyes widened and how they shuffled away as she approached.

"Tessa Hedgehog! You are late and not dressed out in fur yet!" Mr. Grizzly pointed out the obvious, his roar normally one that would make Tessa tremble in fear.

Today, however, it was the last and final straw.

Tessa whirled toward him, a quivering mass of rage. Before she could say anything, though, fifteen more spines broke free from her skin, exploding one after the other in a series of sharp, stabbing pops. "I. Am. *Quilling*!" she shouted at Mr. Grizzly, shaking clenched fists at him.

His eyes widened and he actually took a step back.

"Does no one understand what it means to suffer through the pain and indignity of having *six thousand* spines break through their skin over the course of two months? I'd like to see you get to class on time in this condition!" She swept a hand from her hair to her feet. "Do you not *see* what I am going through?"

A movement just beyond Mr. Grizzly caught her attention and she realized Katrina had just stepped out of the locker room, still in human form. Katrina was really brave like that, ignoring the rules of even the scariest of teachers. Katrina caught her eyes, nodded and made a "keep going" gesture with her hand.

But Tessa's rage was fading away. Fading that is, until another spine popped loose on the back of her hand, for some reason reminding her that Alex had gotten in the way of her final figure eight, making it awkward and imperfect, and all her rage came tumbling back.

It was rather unfortunate that at that very moment, the door to the boys' locker room opened and Alex and Brock tumbled out in their hedgehog forms.

"And you two!" Tessa stormed toward the two hedgies, who froze mid-roll and stared up at her from wide, terrified eyes. "I am sick of tripping all over you. STOP ruining my figure eights. STOP following me around everywhere and STOP making my spines pop out at school!" She turned and stormed toward the girls' locker room. As she passed Katrina, she couldn't help but notice the grin and fierce look of pride on the tiger's face.

Katrina waited until the locker room door swung closed behind Tessa before turning to face the hedgies, who had gained their feet, but were crouched low to the ground, trying to make themselves as small as possible.

Katrina contemplated letting Tessa's statement be the last one on the subject, but she just couldn't let it pass.

She popped her neck and embraced the tiger.

Mason had been predicting this outcome for weeks. He'd told Luis and Sam that Tessa Hedgehog had a lot of rage built up and he didn't want to be around when she finally let loose. He figured it was entirely possible two hedgehogs and maybe the entire school would be sacrificed to her rage when the inevitable happened.

Overall, though, he was rather disappointed. She didn't even lay a hand on Alex or Brock. He eyed the two hedgehogs. Not that she'd needed to. Those two hedgies were still a quivering mass of fear. His nose twitched. Smelly fear.

To be honest, his bunny had been intimidated too. Tessa was kind of scary in her righteous fury.

Mason hopped over to where Luis and Sam were huddled against the back wall, looking rather intimidated.

He was staring at them when the roar reverberated through the room.

Sam and Luis both fell to their bellies, flat as flat could be.

Mason whirled and stared.

Katrina Tiger, who had been standing in human form just minutes before, was now in full-fledged tiger fury and was bearing down on those hedgies like she was going to eat them for breakfast.

He raced toward them, but knew he'd never make it in time.

He wasn't even sure why he thought he could help. Katrina was about a thousand times his size in their shifted forms. Still he didn't want her to have to live with knowing she'd eaten a couple shifters.

He almost tripped over his feet when she came to a skidding stop over the two hedgies, lowered her giant tiger head to theirs, snapped her gleaming fangs at them and roared in their faces.

Mason's nose twitched as the distinct smell of hedgie urine reached him.

Both Alex and Brock curled into tight balls, their spines interlocking into shields of armor.

Mason didn't think that armor would deter Katrina at all. Those spines might look wicked sharp but he had a feeling she could snap them in two if she wanted.

Dead silence filled the room.

Mason hopped a couple hops closer, wondering if he had the courage to turn Katrina's attention his way.

Then Mr. Grizzly said, "Katrina, control your tiger. Now."

Katrina just held her position, staring at the two terrified rolled-up hedgies for a prolonged moment, then with one final snap of her jaws, turned, flicked her tail at them and walked away.

Mason couldn't take his eyes off her.

She was amazing.

seven

equal rights

After that second night at the movies, when they all watched *9 to 5*, life got rather hectic for Amelia.

The Town Council approved her dad's request to host a rescue event, which meant they had three weeks to get ready for it.

The first thing they had to do was move all the animals to the clinic so people could stop by and get to know them in advance of the event. Once the animals were moved, Amelia started working at the clinic before and after school and on the weekends to help care for them and to help screen applicants. For some reason, there was a constant stream of people wanting to adopt Squeakers, who was absolutely not interested in any of them.

As a result, over the next couple weeks, Amelia only got to see her friends at school and at the clinic whenever they came by to hang out or help plan the event.

Still, remembering her vow to turn Felicia into a cat lover, Amelia chose a DVD each morning, which she then conveniently left at the clinic before heading to school. The DVD then served as an excuse to drag Felicia to the clinic in the afternoons.

While Felicia may have believed Amelia's excuse of having forgotten the DVD the first time it happened, she certainly wasn't fooled after that. Still, each day, she just rolled her eyes and accompanied Amelia to the clinic without too much protest.

Upon arrival, Amelia would send Felicia (and Luis when he accompanied his sister) to the cat room while she went to "hunt down" the DVD. Amelia always took her time, giving Felicia and Luis the opportunity to play with the cats and bond with them. It was working too because despite their best intentions, Amelia could tell both Felicia and Luis were falling in love with Mr. Floof and Ms. Poof.

Each night, after returning home from the clinic, Amelia spent a bit of time perusing her DVD collection, trying to pick something enlightening and entertaining for her friends. Although they didn't watch a movie every night (sometimes they went bowling instead), her friends were still moving fairly quickly through some of her best activist movies and documentaries, including *Iron Jawed Angels, Norma Rae, Sisters of '77* and *She's Beautiful When She's Angry.*

She also chose a few of her favorite movies just for fun, like *Alien* (which, according to Felicia, completely freaked everyone out), *Die Hard* and *My Cousin Vinny,* among others.

"Everyone screamed in *Something's Gotta Give,*" Felicia told her one afternoon.

"What? Why? It's a comedy!"

"Yeah, but that crazy Jack guy was in it!" she exclaimed. "Everyone thought he was going to go nuts again."

Amelia couldn't help but laugh. Jack Nicholson for the win again. "So how's Tessa doing? I feel bad because I was supposed to help her and now I've been so busy with the clinic and planning the event, I've only been able to check in with her during biology and she's not really talking to me. Well to anyone, I guess. She just seems to be getting grouchier and quieter every day. Do you know if Alex and Brock are still harassing her?"

"I don't think so."

"Really? Then why isn't she in a better mood?"

"Well. That's just kind of Tessa's personality, you know."

"Huh." Amelia thought about that a minute. "Are you absolutely certain the boys aren't harassing her? I mean, they have almost every single class with her. How can we possibly monitor that?"

"You haven't heard?" Felicia grinned.

"Heard what?"

"Well first of all, Tessa really told those boys off and then Katrina terrified them. Everyone thought that would put a stop to it, but after a couple days, they were up to their old tricks again. So Katrina got a bunch of kids involved and from what I hear, Alex and Brock haven't been able to get anywhere near Tessa because all the girls in their classes are running interference. Even kids in the hallways who don't know Tessa have been getting in Alex and Brock's way so they can't follow her from class to class."

"Wow. Really?"

"Yeah."

"I just want to hug Katrina right now!"

"I wouldn't recommend it."

Amelia laughed. "Okay. Good point."

"But speaking of Katrina, I took my mom to the movies on Saturday and ran into her and Tessa with their moms. We all had the same idea!"

"That's funny." Amelia ignored the pain she always got when people talked about doing things with their moms. She'd never had a mother, not that she could remember anyway, so she had no idea why it still bothered her. You'd think she'd be used to it by now. "What did you guys watch?"

"*9 to 5*. My mom loved it. And you know what happened when we got home later that night?"

"What?"

"My dad asked my mom to bring him a cup of coffee and she told him to get it for himself!"

Amelia didn't know whether to laugh or be horrified. "Oh, wow. W-what did he do?"

"He stared at her like she was some creature from that alien movie, but then you know what?"

"What?"

"He got up and got his own coffee!" Felicia's voice was stunned, like she couldn't even believe it had happened that way.

"Has your mom always gotten his coffee for him?"

"Yeah. Always. I couldn't believe it. And my mom was kind of shellshocked. Like I don't think she really thought things through or maybe she didn't expect him to do it or I don't know. It was just really weird. Like none of us knew how to react because everything was suddenly upside down. My dad even helped her set the table and she didn't ask him to do that!"

"Wow." Amelia honestly didn't know what to say. She'd grown up with a single father who did everything, at least until Amelia was old enough to help. There were no gendered dynamics in their home. Sometimes Amelia cooked. Sometimes he did. Sometimes he got the drinks. Sometimes she did. Sometimes he mowed the lawn and sometimes she did. They shared the load. That's the way it had always been and she couldn't imagine living any other way.

"Yeah. I heard that Katrina's mom was talking about the movie to some of her friends and then on Sunday, a huge group of women went up to the theater and they stayed there all day, watching movie after movie."

"Oh." Amelia wasn't sure if this was good news. She was starting to feel a little worried. Like maybe she'd unleashed something the town wasn't really ready for. Which was just weird. It was the 21st century. If they weren't ready for women's liberation, they were seriously behind the times and needed to catch up with the rest of the country. Uncomfortable and ready for a change of subject, she said, "So. What are you guys going to do tonight?"

"Didn't you bring us a movie?"

"Um, yeah. Yeah, I did."

"So what is it?"

"It's called *A League of Their Own.*"

"Awesome! What's it about?"

"Women playing baseball."

"Cool. What's baseball?"

Over the next week, Amelia heard more and more stories like the one with Felicia's parents. She also noticed that Katrina seemed to be organizing something. She seemed to be everywhere, talking to all the girls in the school. Amelia assumed it had to do with making sure there was someone always available to run interference between Tessa and the idiots.

"Thanks for organizing everything, Katrina," Amelia said to her in technology class one afternoon.

"Shh," Katrina hissed. "Not so loud."

Amelia rolled her eyes. That was just like Katrina, not wanting anyone to know that she actually cared about anything or anyone.

"Okay. I just really wanted to say thanks."

"No worries."

"I'm just so busy right now trying to get ready for the rescue event, I haven't really been able to help out and I feel bad."

Katrina shook her head. "It's all good. We've got it handled. The event's tomorrow, right?"

"Yep."

"That's good. We made it a point to wait until after the event." The bell rang and Katrina stood, grabbing her stuff. "You know, just in case. See you tomorrow." She hurried to the door.

"Wait. What?"

Katrina was already gone though.

Amelia shook her head and hurried out the door, heading for calculus. Just one more class and then it'd be the weekend.

An hour later, she ran into Felicia and Luis at her locker. "Hey, guys."

"Hi," they chorused.

"We wanted to help," Luis said.

"Yeah, you know, with the event, getting set up and everything," Felicia said.

"Are you moving the animals over to Town Hall tonight?" Luis asked.

"No, I think we're going to do all that early tomorrow morning."

"Oh, but you're going to the clinic tonight, right?" Felicia asked.

"Yeah. I wanted to spend time with the animals, playing with them, since you know, most will be going home with new families tomorrow. This is kind of my last chance to spend time with them."

"Can we come too?" Luis asked.

"Sure!"

It was a fun evening. Even better when Luis and Felicia's parents showed up to meet Mr. Floof and Ms. Poof and agreed to let the twins adopt them.

Felicia kept saying, "I don't want anyone else to get them first!"

Amelia couldn't stop smiling. She'd known it was a match made in heaven.

The next day was long and busy with more matches to make.

Amelia was running non-stop, meeting people, talking about the animals, taking applications and working hard to find the perfect family for each of her four-legged friends.

By the end of the day, she was exhausted.

She'd also heard a lot of kids referring to some event next week at school. She wasn't sure, but it seemed like only the girls were talking about it, which made her kind of suspicious. Was this what Katrina had been referring to? How had she missed whatever they had planned?

She kept trying to ask Felicia what was going on, but more and more families kept arriving and she kept getting distracted.

Sunday was busy with the aftermath of the event – filing paperwork, cleaning up the town hall, cleaning out kennels, and so forth. She didn't even have a chance to think about what might or might not be going on at school that week.

The first chance she really had to ask Felicia what was going on was in art class Monday morning and by then, it was too late.

At 9:05 on the dot, every girl in art class, including Felicia, suddenly stood up.

"What's going on?" Amelia whispered.

"Come on!" Felicia tugged on Amelia's arm, so she got up and followed Felicia and the other girls out of the classroom and down the hall.

"What's going on?" she hissed again.

"Shhh. I'll explain later." As they streamed down the hallway, more and more girls came out of classrooms, to join them in their walk through the halls and out the front door.

As soon as they reached the front lawn of the school, Amelia saw that Katrina and Tessa were waiting for them. They both stood by a pickup truck that appeared to be filled with signs. As more and more girls arrived on the front lawn, they all made a beeline for the two girls, who were handing out megaphones and signs and flags.

Amelia whirled toward Felicia. "What is all this?"

"How could you not know?" Felicia looked shocked.

"Know about what?"

"Katrina organized a walk-out in protest."

"In protest of what?"

"Equal rights."

"You're protesting against equal rights?"

"No. I don't think so." Felicia shook her head. "That doesn't sound right."

"Are you protesting *for* equal rights?"

"Maybe. Something like that. Katrina can explain it better."

"So what do you guys want to get out of this?"

Felicia looked stumped. "What do you mean?"

"I mean what are your list of demands? We just walked out of our classes. What do we want them to give us to convince us to go back inside?"

"Equal rights!" One girl said as she marched by, holding up a sign with those very words on it.

"Yes. That," Felicia said. "We want equal rights."

Amelia sighed. "Okay, but what does that mean? I mean, what's not equal right now that we want to be equal?"

Another girl walked by and said, "Equal pay for equal work!"

"That," Felicia said. "That's what we want."

"But we don't get paid to go to school and neither do the boys."

"Katrina!" Felicia shouted. "Oh, come on." She grabbed Amelia's arm and dragged her over to where Katrina and Tessa stood. "Here. You explain to Amelia what we're doing."

Katrina looked surprised. "You don't know? I mean, you're the one who had us watching all those movies. We're marching for equal rights!"

This conversation was moving in circles. Amelia drew in a deep breath for patience, then asked, "But what does that look like?"

"What do you mean?" Katrina asked.

"Well, eventually, you know, Principal Armadillo's going to want to know why we're marching and what we want. So we kind of have to know."

"We want equal rights," Felicia said impatiently.

"Of course we do," Amelia said. "But what does that look like? What's happening at the school that we want to change?"

"Harassment," Tessa said.

Amelia pointed at her. "Okay, now that works. So, what will that change look like?"

Tessa shook her head. "I-I don't know."

Amelia looked at Katrina, who just shrugged. "Don't ask me."

Great.

eight

the quality of men

MR. SLOTH DIDN'T stop his lecture when half his class walked out. He just continued speaking very slowly about ancient shifter civilizations.

Melvin wasn't sure why the girls had all walked out, but he sure wished he was with them. History was so interminably boring.

On the other hand, now that the entire room was male only, all the tension in his shoulders and neck drained away. He no longer had to focus every single moment on trying to restrain his moose. Or really, his peacock, since it was that animal, never seen but quite frequently felt, who loved to force his antlers out in a bid to impress the girls.

And speaking of girls, Melvin was dying to know what they were up to. And why they hadn't invited him or any of the other boys to join them.

The minutes ticked by slowly. He could barely contain his impatience. This was going to be a really long day seeing as it was only 9:20 in the morning.

"Mr. Sloth." Ms. Spider stood in the doorway. "We're to bring all the remaining students to Cafeteria B."

Mr. Sloth slowly stood. "Very well, students. Let's go."

A few minutes later, they entered Cafeteria B, which was located at the front of the school and had an entire wall of windows facing north. Now Melvin knew why they were there. Because through those windows was a perfect view of the front lawn, where it seemed all the girls in the school were currently milling.

"What are the girls up to, up to?" Paulie wondered out loud.

Melvin shrugged. He had no idea, but he was willing to bet whatever it was was a lot more fun than history class. And now that he thought about it, he had the girls to thank for class ending early. Instead of listening to Mr. Sloth's lecture, he was now here, hanging out with his friends, which really wasn't so bad.

"What's Katrina doing?" Luis demanded. He turned to Jake. "Come on. She's your sister. What's she up to?"

"I don't know! What's Felicia up to?" Jake retorted.

Luis shrugged. "Who knows?"

"It's gotta-gotta-gotta be Amelia-Melia's fault," Paulie said.

"Why Amelia?" Melvin asked.

Paulie groaned. "Seri-seriously? Because she's the only human-human around full of weird-weird-weird ideas."

Melvin rolled his eyes. "I'm looking down there and it doesn't look like Amelia's the one in charge. In fact, she's about the only one not carrying a sign of some sort."

"It looks like Katrina's the one handing them out," Mason observed.

"Really?" Jake turned and stared down at his sister.

"Can anyone read the signs?" Sam asked. "I'm trying, but they're too far away."

"'Woman Power.' 'Women Unite.' 'Equal Pay for Equal Work.' 'No Means No.'" Gary Hawk read off some of the signs, pointing to each one as he did so.

"What does that even mean?" Luis demanded.

"I'm pretty sure it means the girls are tired of not being listened to," Ms. Raccoon said, bringing the grumbling in the room to a halt. "In fact, I think I'll go join them." And to the shock of both the students and the male teachers, Ms. Raccoon walked out of the cafeteria, followed by Ms. Crane, Ms. Spider and every other female teacher in the school.

"Great," Mr. Grizzly said. "What are we going to do now?"

"My wife hasn't fixed me a meal in a week," Mr. Fox complained. "Do you think that mess out there has something to do with it?"

"I'm sure it does," Principal Armadillo said. "I'm going to call the mayor. I don't know what else to do."

While the principal called the mayor and everyone waited for him to arrive, the students stood at the window and watched as the female teachers filed out of the building and joined the girls protesting.

They also watched as passing cars slowed, the drivers speaking to one girl or another before either speeding away or parking to join the crowd.

"This is insane-insane," Paulie said.

"I think it's hilarious," Mason said. He'd run out to a science classroom a few minutes ago and had returned with a pair of binoculars he now had trained on the crowds below. "I'd be willing to bet Paulie's right and somehow Amelia's strange, human ideas led to this. But she looks about as confused as we are, which means someone took her wacky ideas and made them even wackier." He moved the binoculars and trained them on another portion of the crowd. "And I bet I know who that someone is."

Melvin was pretty sure he knew too, and when Jake growled low in his throat, that just cinched it.

Mason jumped, then offered the binoculars to Jake. "Here. Take a look."

Jake grabbed them.

A commotion at the entrance to the cafeteria caught their attention.

Mayor Peacock walked in the door, followed by Joe Grizzly, the P.E. teacher's brother and a member of the Town Council.

"David, Joe. Thanks for coming," Principal Armadillo said. "Couldn't Maggie and Jessica join you?"

"Oh, they're here," Mayor Peacock said and he pointed to the windows.

Melvin looked out and sure enough, the missing Council Members, Jessica Canary and Maggie Fox, were down in the crowds, joining the resistance.

"Great," Principal Armadillo said in disgust. "What are we going to do?"

"Isn't it obvious-obvious?" Paulie exclaimed.

Everyone stared at him.

"Get Amelia-Melia to make them stop-stop."

"Paulie." Melvin shook his head.

"I'm just saying-saying! She's the one with all the wacky-wacky ideas."

Mayor Peacock nodded. "The kid's right. How about if we call Amelia's dad, get him to come to the school. I bet he can help end this nonsense."

Melvin grinned. He didn't really know George Finch that well, but if he was anything like his daughter, Melvin could pretty much predict his response wouldn't be anything like what the Town Council expected.

Twenty minutes later, Mr. Finch wandered into the cafeteria. "Mayor Peacock, Principal Armadillo. Thought I'd never get through all the traffic out there." He glanced around the room. "You boys aren't joining the classes outside today?"

"George." Principal Armadillo walked over to him. "Thanks for coming, but those aren't classes."

"No? Has school let out already?"

"No, it has not. Your daughter, Amelia, led all our female students outside where they are now marching for equal rights."

"Really?" Mr. Finch hurried over to the window. "Why, I guess they do have signs, don't they? It's a picket line! How wonderful."

"They interrupted classes, George!"

Mr. Finch didn't reply, just continued staring outside. "That girl," he said. His voice was full of affection.

Melvin moved to the right a little so he could see Mr. Finch's face. He was grinning from ear to ear.

"Always involved," Mr. Finch said. "Always fighting for the right causes." He glanced over his shoulder at the principal and mayor. "I'm so glad you brought me down here. She didn't tell me she'd organized something like this. Amelia's not one to toot her own horn, but this is amazing."

Melvin had a hard time controlling his laughter. The look on Principal Armadillo's face was priceless. And Mayor Peacock's face was turning bright red.

David Peacock was in shock. George's reaction was unbelievable! If David didn't know any better, he'd think George was actually proud of his daughter for this nonsense!

George turned back to the windows. "To think she rallied not just the teens, but all the women in town." He peered closer. "I think she even got Debbie involved."

David hurried over to look. All the students crowded around to see.

George was right!

Debbie Panda was out there marching with the women.

George hurried to the door.

"Wait! Where are you going?" Steve Armadillo asked.

"Where do you think? I'm gonna join my baby girl on the protest line. Never let it be said that George Finch was too selfish to march for women's rights." And he disappeared out the door.

The room was dead silent, everyone in shock, then Paulie Porcupine cracked up. He leaned against the wall, chortling and snorting with laughter.

Many of the other students started laughing as well.

Melvin Moose laughed so hard, David spent a moment worrying about exploding antlers, then realized there were only men and boys in the room, so they were probably safe.

"Well, that went really well," Joe Grizzly said.

"Smashingly," his brother, Karl, said.

"You know what this means, don't you?" David asked. The ramifications were mind-boggling. He couldn't believe how much trouble one teenaged human girl had become. She'd actually rallied adults to her ridiculous cause.

"What does it mean?" Steve asked.

"It means we're all going to have to change."

"Change? Change how?" Joe exclaimed.

David shook his head. "I'm not sure. I think we'll have to get Amelia's help on this one, but basically, I think we're going to all have to learn to be better men."

"But we're not men," Alex protested. "We're shifters!"

"Yeah," Brock said indignantly.

Great. Now they had a budding revolt from the boys as well. David felt completely out of his depth.

Thankfully, though, they had an armadillo principal who had a lot of experience dealing with unruly teenaged boys. "Well, I'm sorry to contradict you, Alex and Brock, but we are in fact men," Steve said. "We may have animals inside, but at the end of the day, it's the quality of the men we are that determine the lives we lead. And don't think for one minute that I don't know you two are the reason we're all in this fix. Constantly bothering young Tessa. You should be ashamed of yourselves!"

"But we were just showing her our appreciation," Brock exclaimed.

"Yeah," Alex said. "We're hedgehogs. It's what we do!"

"That's ridiculous," Melvin said before Steve had a chance to respond. "I struggle every day to control my antlers. I may not be good at it yet, but I'm giving it my best effort. You two aren't even trying!"

David could see astonishment and dawning pride on all the teachers' faces. Clearly they never expected much from the boy. David wasn't surprised though. After what had happened at the rescue event over the weekend, he would never underestimate Melvin Moose again.

As for Brock and Alex, they both looked crestfallen.

"But–" Alex began.

Melvin shook his head. "No excuses."

Jake Tiger stepped up to stand beside Melvin. "He's right. No excuses." Jake then turned to face the principal. "I'm going outside, sir, to join my sister."

Luis Rabbit stepped forward. "Me too."

Melvin grinned. "Well, I'd go with you both, but …" He gestured at his head where David knew antlers were sure to grow if Melvin joined the crowd of females outside.

Luis and Jake laughed.

"It's the thought that counts," Jake said.

Luis nodded and the two boys walked out together.

Sam and Mason Rabbit, Devon Raccoon and a slew of other boys followed them out.

"Well, that's just great!" Brock exclaimed.

Alex huffed. "I guess we're going to have to apologize."

"Yeah." Brock looked disgusted.

"Well, come on, then. I'm not doing this alone." Alex grabbed Brock's arm and dragged him out the door.

Mr. Fox sighed. "I guess I should accompany my students. I do not like this turn of events though." He stomped out, the rest of the male staff members following him.

Mr. Sloth chuckled. "Personally," he said as he moved slowly toward the door in their wake. "I've found this year to be so much fun."

"I have to agree," Karl Grizzly said as he matched his step to Mr. Sloth's. "It's certainly been more interesting than any other school year I've experienced and I was here when Karly Bat and Lexie Mosquito were dating and then broke up. Oh, the uproar."

The sound of their laughter trailed behind them as they disappeared out the door.

nine

paying the price

AMELIA WASN'T EXACTLY sure it was a good thing when their female teachers joined them on the picket line, especially after Ms. Crane cornered her and demanded to know what "equal pay for equal work" meant.

When Amelia explained, Ms. Crane just stared at her, then called Ms. Spider over so Amelia could explain again. By the time she'd explained the concept for the third time in a row, there was a huge group of women around her, debating their salaries. As the debate raged, it became clear to Amelia that there really was no gender disparity when it came to salaries in Shifferville. Salaries were set according to the job a person did and it didn't matter their gender.

The more Amelia lived in this town, the weirder she found it. There were just so many discrepancies. No wage gap, but a huge majority of the women did all the cooking and cleaning in the home. No tolerance for animal cruelty, but nobody blinked at sexual harassment.

"Amelia, there you are!"

"Dad, what are you doing here?"

"Principal Armadillo called me, told me you'd arranged all this. I'm so proud of you, sweetheart."

"Actually, it wasn't me. It was really Katrina. You remember her?"

"The one with the bunny for a pet?"

"Yep."

"Well, this is pretty impressive, no matter who organized it." He leaned over and murmured, "Not sure why, but Principal Armadillo's pretty sure you're to blame."

Amelia rolled her eyes. "Well, I guess I kind of am. I mean I have been sharing a lot of my ideas and my movies and… yeah."

Her dad chuckled. "That's my girl. Well, I'm going to go chat with Debbie. I gave her the day off to make up for all the extra hours she's been putting in, preparing for the rescue event, and look at her now. Picketing on her day off!" He walked away.

Amelia wandered over to Katrina. "My dad was really impressed, Katrina."

"He was?"

"Yep."

"Amelia Finch!"

"Oh, boy," Katrina said. "Principal Armadillo's on the warpath." She began to edge away.

"Oh, no." Amelia grabbed her sleeve. "You planned this, you get to face him with me."

"While this is all extremely impressive, young lady, it's also very distracting and isn't helping any of these young people gain the education they need." Principal Armadillo began his lecture before he even reached them. "So." He came to a halt in front of Amelia. "Tell me exactly what you want so we can get this show on the road and school back in session."

"Well," Amelia said, "actually, sir, I didn't arrange all this. I think Katrina's the one who has some demands. Katrina and–" she looked around, threw out an arm and snagged a sleeve, "–Tessa." She dragged Tessa over to their group. "Go on, ladies, tell him what we're picketing for."

"Tessa." Katrina looked at her expectantly.

"Well. Um." Tessa looked around wildly.

Amelia gave her a quick nod and a nudge. "Go on," she whispered.

"Equal rights," Tessa blurted out. "I don't like it when the boys are always harassing me. I don't harass them. They don't have to deal with someone following them. Everywhere. From place to place. All the time. I want to be treated like I treat them. With respect."

"I think that sounds reasonable," Principal Armadillo said. "So no–what did you call it?

"Harassment," Tessa said.

"Right. No harassment. What else?"

Tessa threw a wild look at Katrina, who just shrugged. She had no ideas.

"I think maybe that's it," Katrina said.

Tessa nodded in agreement.

"No, that is not it!" Ms. Crane stormed over to stand beside the girls. "These girls would also like the men of this town to agree that it isn't just the women's job to cook and clean for their households. Men live there so they can contribute too."

"Yes, that's right," Katrina said quickly. "Equal rights."

"Yes, equal rights!" exclaimed Tessa.

"Equal rights!" shouted all the women around them. "Equal rights, equal rights!"

"All right, all right, all right!" Principal Armadillo yelled, but he wasn't heard for all the shouting. He turned to Felicia. "Can I borrow your megaphone?"

Felicia looked down at it, then over at Katrina.

Katrina nodded, so Felicia handed it over.

Principal Armadillo checked the volume, then announced, "Teachers, please escort your students to the gym where I'll be making an announcement shortly."

It took quite a bit of time to get everyone organized and moving back into the building.

There was a sense of excitement in the air as both teachers and students anticipated a major policy change was imminent. Amelia noticed that all the adults who had joined the protest, adults who weren't even teachers at the school, still filed in with all the students, clearly curious to see what the protest had achieved.

Once everyone was seated on the bleachers, Principal Armadillo called the gathering to order. "Ahem. Okay, so, ladies and gentlemen, it has come to my attention that we've had an issue with harassment at this school. Now, in case you are unaware of what that term means…" he cleared his throat, "I'm going to let Amelia Finch explain it to you."

Amelia's eyes got wide. "What?"

"Go on, Amelia," Felicia gave her a nudge.

This was so not cool.

Realizing she had no other choice, Amelia slowly made her way to where Principal Armadillo stood.

He handed her the megaphone and she stared at it a moment, then with a big sigh, lifted it and said, "Look, harassment is just when you're bothering someone who doesn't want to be bothered. I'll give you some examples. If you're following someone and they say don't follow me and you keep following them, that's harassment. If you want to kiss someone and they don't want to kiss you and you kiss them anyway, that's harassment."

Murmurs rippled through the bleachers.

"If you like someone and you call them or text them or send them emails all the time and refuse to stop even after they ask you to, that's harassment." She looked at Principal Armadillo, started to hand him the megaphone, then changed her mind and added, "Don't do it. If you harass someone, you're a jerk, and no one likes a jerk."

She handed the megaphone to the principal and walked off. She didn't bother going back to her spot in the bleachers because she was afraid she might be called back down to the floor and wasn't in the mood to keep trekking up and down them.

"All right, then, so there you have it. Shift–" Principal Armadillo broke into a coughing fit, holding up a finger to indicate everyone needed to wait a moment. When he had his cough under control, he said, "Shiffer High is now implementing a no harassment policy. If someone asks you to leave them alone, you need to respect their request."

"But how are we supposed to show our appreciation?" someone called out.

Amelia groaned. She just knew it had to be one of the idiots.

"You need to act like civilized boys and girls," Principal Armadillo said.

"What does that mean though? How will someone know I like them if I'm acting all civilized?"

Amelia wasn't sure who called out that question, but it was pretty disgusting on the whole.

"Well, I imagine you just tell that person you're interested in them," Principal Armadillo replied.

A burst of sound rippled through the gym as the students began to chatter about this concept.

"Tell them?"

"Sounds boring!" Someone shouted.

A lot of the students laughed.

"I'd rather impress them with my figure eights," Alex shouted.

Several other students called out their preferences, at which point Principal Armadillo lost his temper. "Look! If Melvin Moose can–" he broke off and threw a wild look at Amelia. He cleared his throat. "I mean, you aren't children anymore. You're young men and women and you can learn to control yourselves, so do it!" He shouted the last few words. "Now everyone back to class. You have 5 minutes to make it to your 4th hour class. No running. Go."

As the students surged around Amelia, she wondered exactly what Principal Armadillo had been going to say before he broke off. If Melvin Moose could – what? What could Melvin do that had the principal calling it out in front of the entire school, but then not actually finishing his sentence because Amelia was there?

This had happened entirely too many times. Amelia was out of excuses for her friends, for the teachers, for the high school, for the entire town. There was some huge secret these people were keeping from her and she was going to figure it out. No matter how long it took.

"Well, that's just great," someone growled.

Amelia froze. While she'd been standing there, the gym had emptied out and she now stood alone, in the shadow of one of the bleachers. She crept further beneath them to peek out at the main floor.

The entire town council – Mayor Peacock, Principal Armadillo, Maggie Fox, Jessica Canary and Joe Grizzly – was standing at the center of the gym.

Amelia held her breath, waiting in terrified anticipation of what she might overhear.

"You almost gave us away to the human, Steve," Joe Grizzly growled.

"I know, but you guys have no idea how difficult this job is!" Principal Armadillo exclaimed. "Every day, trying to keep that girl from discovering something she shouldn't. Keeping her away from all the extra cafeterias, from P.E. class, from entire sections of the school. I mean what if she wanders into the wrong biology class or the *other* library? We're screwed, guys. There's no way we're keeping this from her long-term. This was the dumbest idea we ever had."

"I know," Maggie said. "I knew it at the time. We all knew it. What were we thinking?"

"We were desperate," Jessica said.

Principal Armadillo nodded. "Frantic and desperate."

"And now we're paying the price," Mayor Peacock said.

"And at some point," Joe said, "the humans will undoubtedly have to pay it too."

The five council members trooped out of the gym, leaving Amelia standing beneath the bleachers, hands clamped over her mouth, trembling in frozen silence.

The Trouble With Humans (a.k.a. They're Not Shifters)

Shifter High: Season 1, Episode 5

Written By

A.J. CULEY

CONTENTS

"This job is impossible!
I've got predators stalking prey in the halls,
exploding antlers and now a human to worry about!"
- Principal Armadillo

"Amelia's suspicious and I'm tired.
Tired of keeping secrets from my best friend."
-Felicia Rabbit

"Amelia's not an idiot.
She's going to figure things out.
Exposure is inevitable.
And I'm okay with that.
As long as I'm not the one doing the exposing."
- Melvin Moose

"All I really have to say is
WHAT. THE. HELVETICA?"
- Amelia Finch

one

aliens

AMELIA FINCH BOLTED across the gymnasium floor to a side door she was hoping would lead outside.

School wasn't out yet. She was supposed to be in her fourth hour class, but there was no way she was staying for the rest of the day. Not after what she'd just heard.

She needed time to think.

Away from her friends.

Away from this school.

Relief coursed through her when she opened the door and sunlight poured in. She slipped through and let it close behind her.

A huge field stretched in front of her, running from the gymnasium at her back toward the front of the school. To her left was one long wall of windows, classrooms facing the field she'd have to cross to get to the front of the school to begin the long walk home.

Staring out at the field, wondering how she'd traverse it without being seen, a flash of memory froze her.

Closing her eyes, Amelia tried to picture the school. The long hallways, the cafeteria, the gymnasium at her back, the classrooms overlooking this field.

Art.

Her eyes flew open.

Though she had no idea which classrooms were on the upper floors, she was pretty sure her first floor art classroom was on this side of the building.

Which meant the windows she'd stared out of during class looked out across this field.

Where she'd once seen a tiger running by.

Oh, her friends had tried to convince her she'd imagined things, but since the entire town operated as an animal preserve, Amelia'd been sure they were lying to her.

Now, after overhearing the Town Council's conversation in the gym, she no longer had any doubts.

It *had* been a tiger.

Which meant Amelia was now in its territory.

Whirling around, she yanked on the gym door's handle, but it was locked.

Damn.

Now she not only had to worry about not being seen by the teachers in the classrooms, but also by the tiger someone had apparently let loose on school grounds.

Of course, that had been at least a month ago and she hadn't seen any tigers since then, so maybe the tiger had moved on.

Or maybe the townspeople had caught it and returned it to wherever tigers lived in this wacky town.

Or not.

Either way, she really needed to get out of there. She'd seen her dad in the gymnasium when Principal Armadillo made his announcement. Maybe she could catch him before he left. He could take her home, where she'd be safe.

Away from everyone.

Where she could think in peace about what she'd overheard.

Not that she really wanted to.

She'd been perfectly happy thinking everyone in Shifferville was just a little odd or that they were members of some strange animal-worshipping cult. Though she'd never really been satisfied with either of those explanations, she'd been willing to accept them, *because they were sane.*

This though. This new development.

Amelia let out a huff of exasperation and, without allowing herself to think about the tiger that may or may not be on the loose or the students and teachers who may or may not be staring out their classroom windows right that very minute, stalked across the field.

Remembering how Mr. Grizzly (the Town Council member, not the P.E. teacher) had growled at Principal Armadillo and accused him of nearly giving everything away to *the human*, she broke into a run, her bookbag banging against her hip with every movement.

Why did they keep calling her that? Everywhere she went, she heard that word, *human,* and not in a generic, talking-about-humanity kind of way.

At this point, the only conclusion Amelia could come to was that the Town Council, her classmates, maybe even the other residents in town, weren't human. It was completely ridiculous, of course, and yet, in a really weird way, it was the only thing that made sense. The only thing that explained everything she'd seen so far *and* the conversation she'd just overheard.

Her friends weren't human, just like the tiger she'd seen wasn't human.

The tiger!

"Mr. Raccoon! What exactly are you staring at?"

Devon startled at Ms. Spider's demand and dragged his eyes away from the window, though he didn't really want to miss what was happening outside. "Oh, um, sorry, it's just–" He turned back to the window and stared as Amelia stopped running to spin around in a circle, then stare off into the woods.

"What's the human doing out there?" Sally Ostrich asked over his shoulder.

Gasping for breath, Amelia whirled around and scanned the field, horrified that she'd been running when there was a tiger out there. What if she'd triggered its hunting instincts?

Thankfully, the tiger wasn't anywhere that she could see.

Though it could be in the woods.

She shuddered and slowly turned to stare at the woods that ran along the far side of the field.

What if it was crouched in the shadows of the trees right now?

Watching her.

Stalking her.

Getting ready to pounce.

Gritting her teeth, she began to walk again.

Slowly.

Don't run. Don't run.

"That is disgusting." Jake Tiger had a high tolerance for food prep, but this was the most disgusting thing he'd ever seen. He'd enrolled in Culinary Arts for Carnivores as a means of gaining additional meat throughout the school day, not so he'd have to watch a polar bear slaughter a seal.

"I agree," Victor Hyena said. "How can she stand to smell that, let alone eat it?"

They'd already had to watch Kayla Polar extract the seemingly endless intestines from the seal, then butcher the carcass into cubes of meat. And now they were forced to watch as she braided the intestines she'd extracted.

"Why doesn't she just throw it away?" Victor groaned. "It smells disgusting."

"I think we're supposed to cook it. And *eat* it." Jake couldn't even imagine such a thing, but Kayla's bear always seemed super close to the surface, so she might not mind the idea. He expected polars in the wild probably ate every bit of the seal.

Kayla's fingers wove in and out of the long piece of intestine, creating knot after knot until it was entirely braided. She looked up with a huge smile on her face. "It's ready for boiling, Mr. Macaque."

"Excellent, Kayla." Mr. Macaque stepped over to the trio and raised an eyebrow at the boys.

Jake nodded, steeled himself and stepped closer to the stench of seal. He lifted the lid on the pot of boiling water and watched as Kayla dropped the braided intestine inside.

"Hey, you guys. What do you think the human's doing down there?" Paulo Komodo asked.

The further she walked, the angrier Amelia got.

Stupid tiger freaking her out, stalking her from the woods.

Eventually, she couldn't help it and started to jog again, before slowing back down to a walk, then jogging a bit more.

Worried the tiger might come up behind her, she swung around and jogged backward for a bit before turning and running forward again.

She spun in a circle a couple times, trying to keep her eyes continually roaming the entire field, just in case the tiger came back.

She had no idea how she would defend herself against a tiger, but didn't want to be taken by surprise.

If nothing else, she wanted to see death coming.

"Um, Mr. Pterodactyl?" Gary Hawk hesitantly raised his hand.

"Do you have a question about wind velocity, Mr. Hawk?"

"No, sir."

"Are you curious about anything related to shifter aerodynamics, Mr. Hawk?"

"Well, no, sir, but I *am* curious about what the human's doing down there." Gary pointed to the field far below.

Eddie Macaw snickered.

They'd both been watching the human for a while now, rather than paying attention to class, even though they'd been super excited when they came out on the roof, ready for another flight lesson.

The human was way more interesting than Mr. Pterodactyl's safety lecture though.

She'd freaked out when she'd realized she was locked out of the building and ever since had been in this weird pattern of run, walk, spin, throw arms in the air, and then repeat.

Gary wasn't sure, but he also thought she might have been talking to herself the entire time.

"What are you going on about?" Mr. Pterodactyl joined Gary at the edge of the roof, stared down at the human for a moment, then propped his hands on his hips and sighed.

"Humans are so weird," Eddie Macaw muttered as they watched Amelia jump up and down in place and yell something at the woods.

"What do you think she's saying?" Sabeen Kingfisher asked.

"And is anyone replying or is she just crazy?" Mandy Turaco said.

Amelia stopped again.

She could feel the tiger's eyes on her. Maybe even more than one tiger's eyes.

"Well come on then!" She whirled to face the woods and threw her arms in the air. "If you're not going to attack me, I don't have time for this. So come on! Let's go!"

What was she doing? Had she gone completely mad? Inciting a tiger to attack. She *was* mad!

But her friends might not be human! Who cared about tigers when she was human and her friends were *not*.

Hands on hips, Amelia stared into the woods and spoke the words out loud, as if that might somehow bring sanity to an insane situation. "My friends aren't human."

She closed her eyes, dropped her head and pondered those words.

What did not human even mean?

Not human *how*?

She began to pace back and forth as she debated the possibilities.

"Okay, so they're not human. Aliens?" Didn't Felicia say they all freaked out at the movie *Alien?* Amelia wished she'd watched it with them, so she'd know whether they'd freaked out at the birth scene (anyone would have) or if they'd simply freaked out at the idea of aliens because if it was the latter, that probably meant they *weren't* aliens.

But if not aliens, what?

"Vampires?" Amelia couldn't believe she'd entertained the thought, let alone said it out loud.

"Here's hoping for aliens," she muttered as she swung around and began to jog toward the front of the building once more.

Aliens before vampires.

Always.

Aliens wouldn't explain the tiger though.

Or Victor Hyena and his obsession with sniffing her hair and calling her prey.

On the other hand, maybe it would.

She skidded to a halt and raked her hands through her hair.

The memory of an old TV mini-series her dad had on DVD flashed through her head. Hadn't the aliens been lizards or something like that? Dressed in human skin?

Holy megabytes.

Aliens might explain everything.

"What is she *doing*?" Rosa Armadillo exclaimed. She was supposed to be heading to the front of the room to give her report on the psychology of the Hybrid Effect, but she'd glanced out the window on her way and now she was riveted.

The rest of the class crowded around her to stare down from the second floor windows.

The human was walking in circles! And–

"Is she talking to herself? Do humans do that? Talk to nobody?" Rosa looked over her shoulder at Ms. Squirrel, who looked rather surprised herself.

"I think at least some humans do," Shane Wolf said. "That's what that crazy Jack character did."

"Oh, great," Akemi Serow muttered. "If she starts talking about being a good girl, I'm leaving town."

Rosa looked back out the window, just in time to see Amelia stop again, hands on hips before throwing up her arms and walking some more.

"Why is she flapping her arms?" Mateo Jaguar asked.

"Oooh! Maybe she's a shifter after all!" Rosa exclaimed. "Maybe she's going to shift into a finch!"

"Don't be ridiculous," Ms. Squirrel said. "That girl smells entirely 100% human."

"True," Mateo said. "It's actually quite sad. No animal at all."

"Yeah," Shane said. "I don't know how humans stand it."

"They must be so lonely," Rosa whispered.

"All right, all right." Ms. Squirrel waded into the group and started ushering students back to their desks. "While I do agree the human would be an excellent test study, especially when it comes to her very bizarre behavior," Ms. Squirrel paused to think about that a moment before shaking her head to continue, "right now everyone needs to settle down so we can hear Rosa's report on *shifter* psychology. Rosa?"

Amelia stopped jogging to pace and debate the entire thing in her head some more.

Vampires made no sense.

But aliens.

Aliens could look like anything.

Right?

They could probably sound like anything too.

Maybe aliens would explain Katrina Tiger's freaky eyes and her striped hair. Also her tendency to growl. Maybe that's what aliens looked and sounded like on her home planet.

Maybe they'd also explain Paulie Porcupine's obsession with digging and Felicia Rabbit's constant bouncing. Maybe that's how aliens acted on their planets.

Except.

Now they weren't just from one planet, but from many? All in one town?

That made no sense at all.

But it was still better than vampires.

She started walking again, no longer even worried about the tiger.

Now she had to figure out how to prove the town was full of aliens.

Either that or just let it go and continue pretending everything was normal and never learn the truth.

Amelia shook her head.

Not a chance.

"Want me to go down and spy on her?" Gary asked Mr. Pterodactyl. It would be really cool if he said yes. Then Gary could practice soaring on the breeze while also appeasing his curiosity about the human and what exactly she was going on about. Because there was no doubt about it – she was definitely talking to someone. So Mandy's question was a really good one.

Was anyone replying to Amelia Human?

Mr. Pterodactyl sighed. "No. We'll just wait. It looks like her dad's still here. Hopefully they'll leave soon and we can finally get off the ground for a flight lesson."

"I'm hungry," Eddie said.

"Yeah, we didn't get lunch today! That's so wrong," Sabeen said.

"It's your fault we didn't get to eat," Zack Eagle snorted. "All you girls took up our lunch period."

"No one's going to starve," Mr. Pterodactyl said. "Everything just got a little behind today. As soon as lunch is ready, they'll ring the bell."

As if his words made it happen, the bell rang at that exact moment, making everyone laugh.

"All right then," Mr. Pterodactyl said. "Off you go. We'll continue this lesson after lunch."

Amelia rounded the side of the building and and squinted toward the front parking lot. Was that her dad?

It was.

He stood next to their car, facing Debbie Panda, who was talking to him and smiling.

Amelia hurried forward, shocked to realize her dad seemed to actually be *engaged* in the conversation.

When did her dad ever look at someone while they were talking? Well, he did with her, but not anyone else. No one else was really worth his time. Amelia and animals. That was all her dad was really into.

Until now.

Debbie Panda, with her white hair that had black patches over her ears, had somehow managed to catch his attention.

Debbie Panda.

Who might be an alien.

Amelia walked slowly toward the pair, noting how they leaned toward each other just a little and how they were both smiling.

She scowled. She wanted her dad to be happy, but she had no idea at all what kind of dangerous *creature* Debbie might be.

Amelia winced at the thought and stopped, raking her hands through her hair in frustration.

Debbie'd always been nice to Amelia. Even when Amelia hadn't been very nice to her. Did it matter if she wasn't human? If she was an alien? Or whatever?

Amelia really wanted to say that it didn't matter. She didn't avoid people just because they were different. But this was way more different than she'd ever experienced before.

They weren't human!

And they were keeping that truth under wraps. The truth of who they really were.

If Debbie Panda was interested in Amelia's dad, she was going to have to be honest about who she was.

No more secrets!

two

the truth

"WHERE'S THE HUMAN?"

Felicia Rabbit startled badly at Jake Tiger's voice, fumbling her phone. When had the Tigers come into the bowling alley? She hadn't heard them or smelled them!

She glanced around wildly and saw that her brother, Luis, and cousin, Sam, had leapt away from where they'd been standing and were now pretending to bowl, far away from Felicia and the Tigers.

Traitors!

"Well?" Jake demanded.

She cleared her throat. "Um, I don't think she's coming."

"Why not?" Katrina Tiger asked.

"I think she left school early. She wasn't at lunch," Felicia said.

"Or in biology class," Tessa Hedgehog said. At least Tessa hadn't abandoned Felicia!

Katrina nodded. "She wasn't in computer programming either."

Jake grunted. "She was definitely acting weird after the assembly today."

"You saw her?" Felicia asked.

"Not really." He didn't say anything else.

What did that mean? How did he know she was acting weird if he hadn't even seen her? Before Felicia could decide whether she wanted to try to get more information out of a surly tiger, her phone buzzed. She glanced down and could feel the blood draining from her face as she read Amelia's text. "I knew it! She knows."

"Knows what?" Mason asked. He was the only bunny still standing with them, though he was now closer to Katrina than Felicia. That crazy rabbit had no sense of self-preservation.

"You know," Felicia said. "She *knows.*"

"What?" Katrina exclaimed. "How do you know that?"

"She's not coming." Felicia held up her phone. "She just texted that she wasn't feeling well and she'll see me tomorrow."

"Good," Jake said and he walked away.

Felicia's jaw dropped. "Did he just say good?"

Katrina rolled her eyes. "Forget about him. Why do you say Amelia knows?"

"Yeah, how come?" Luis abandoned his bowling to inch closer, though he kept Felicia's body between his and Katrina's.

Sad and pathetic.

Felicia glared at him.

"What?" He stopped and glared back.

"Well if you don't know–"

"I don't. That's why I asked."

How could he not know? He was her brother! He should be protecting her from the Tigers, not using her as a shield. Not that Katrina would ever hurt Felicia, but still!

"Felicia." Katrina sounded impatient.

Luis stumbled back, leaving his sister to face Katrina all alone.

Again!

Such a coward.

"What?" Felicia asked.

"Why do you say that Amelia knows?"

"She just does, okay? Something happened today. She didn't go to classes after our walk-out and she didn't come to lunch and now she's not feeling well? Staying at home? Something happened. She *knows*."

"She doesn't know," Luis said.

Felicia didn't bother looking back at him. She could tell by the tone of his voice that he was rolling his eyes at her, but she didn't care what he thought.

He'd failed to protect her from the Tigers!

Not that she needed protecting, but still!

"That's it?" Katrina demanded flatly. "Because she's skipping classes and not coming to bowl, you're convinced she knows?"

"Sure. Plus she sounded weird in her text."

"Well, what did she say?"

Felicia pulled up the text again and read it out loud. "Not feeling well. See you tomorrow."

There was a beat of silence, then Katrina said, "That's it?"

Felicia nodded.

"That's a perfectly normal sounding text!" Tessa said. She glanced around. "Isn't it?"

"Yes," Luis said decisively. "Felicia's just paranoid. As usual."

"I'm not paranoid, Luis Rabbit!" Felicia whirled on her brother. "I'm just concerned. What happens if–"

A loud bang made them all jump.

Felicia whirled around again.

Two figures stood in the doorway to the bowling alley. The sunlight behind them cast them in shadow, so she couldn't tell who they were at first, just that one figure was much taller than the other.

They both stepped forward, the door closed behind them and she realized it was Melvin Moose and Paulie Porcupine.

"What are you two doing here?" Tessa sounded shocked.

"What do you mean-mean-mean?" Paulie asked defensively. "So we can't bowl-bowl-bowl now either?"

"Calm down, Paulie," Melvin said. "Jake texted and said Amelia's not bowling tonight."

Everyone looked over at Jake, who was bowling by himself at a lane across the room.

After launching a ball that hurtled down the lane and knocked over all the pins, Jake turned and shrugged. "It may be his only chance to bowl with us."

"Who cares about bowling?" Felicia asked. "I'm telling you guys Amelia knows."

Jake froze in the act of reaching for another ball. He slowly turned to face Felicia, making her inner bunny want to dive into a burrow and hide. "What do you mean she knows?"

"She just does, okay. I can tell."

"Well, how is that even possible?" Katrina demanded.

After a beat of silence, everyone turned to look at Melvin, who held up his hands. "Hey, I've been good. She hasn't caught even a glimpse of my moose or my antlers, so if she found out, it wasn't because of me. To be honest, though, I wish she would find out, then I could stop worrying about it."

"How can you even say that, Melvin?" Felicia wailed. "The adults won't like it if the humans learn our secret. Can you imagine what they'll do to Amelia if she finds out?"

Melvin rolled his eyes. "It's not like they'll kill her, so…"

Silence.

He laughed. "Aw, come on. You don't seriously think–"

"No one's ever found out about us before, at least that we know of," Jake said quietly. "In the history of the world, have any of you ever heard of one single human knowing about us?"

After a moment, everyone shook their head.

"In the entire history of the world, not one single human," Jake repeated.

More silence.

"Yeah. I'm pretty sure shifters have a long history of killing humans who discover the truth."

"How do you figure?" Katrina asked.

"Well, you know, don't you think there'd be stories in our history books of humans discovering the truth and what happened? Instead, there are no stories, which has to mean those humans found out and never had a chance to do anything about it."

"Maybe no one ever-ever found out about us, about us," Paulie suggested.

"In thousands of years of human history?" Jake asked dryly. "Doubtful."

"We have to protect her," Felicia exclaimed.

"We need a plan," Katrina said.

"You guys are fighting the inevitable," Melvin said. "She's not stupid. Eventually, one of these days, she's going to figure things out."

"Someone's gonna have to keep an eye on her," Jake said. "Probably a lot of someones."

"What's that gonna do?" Mason asked.

"You're right. They'll have to do more than just watch," Jake said. "We need an entire system in place to keep Amelia from going where she shouldn't, to keep her from stumbling on the truth."

Amelia spent the evening writing notes about what she'd heard in the gymnasium and decided she'd start with Principal Armadillo's rant about all the places at school he had to keep the *human* from visiting.

He'd mentioned extra cafeterias, P.E., a different biology class and the *other* library, which actually was the most interesting to her (an entire library she hadn't yet discovered, full of books she'd probably never read before – she couldn't wait!)

Still, since she had no idea where this secret library was located, she should probably start with someplace a bit easier to find, though not P.E. class. Mr. Grizzly had made it clear on her first day that she wasn't welcome there and honestly, she found him to be just a little terrifying.

So she'd start with the extra cafeterias, which shouldn't be too hard to find. All she'd have to do is follow the students.

The ones who didn't eat in Cafeteria A, that is.

Though she'd have to pretend to head there, at least until Ms. Saber went back inside her classroom.

It had taken days for Ms. Saber to trust Amelia to make it to lunch on her own and weeks for her to stop reminding Amelia that she was to head straight to Cafeteria A, nowhere else. At the time, Ms. Saber's insistence had seemed a little strange, but now Amelia realized it was more than that. It was another piece in the conspiracy puzzle, one that everyone but her was in on, and she was going to figure it out.

As Amelia lay in bed that night, she contemplated various reasons the extra cafeterias might be off limits to humans, and really couldn't come up with a single one that wasn't somewhat alarming. To make matters worse, a sudden memory of the TV lizards harvesting humans for food flashed through her mind just as she was drifting off to sleep.

The result was a restless night filled with uneasy dreams of alien mother ships manned by Shiffer High students dressed in red uniforms.

Amelia woke with a vague memory of standing in an alien cafeteria watching as Victor Hyena gulped down a squirming white mouse and Katrina Tiger a huge guinea pig that bulged from her throat on its way down her gullet.

Clearly Amelia's subconscious had fully embraced the idea of aliens, melding her memories of the classic mini-series *V* with that of her classmates' vaguely predatory airs.

This was not a happy development for Amelia. She fully intended to find those extra cafeterias, but now that her dreams had been filled with nightmare images of humans on serving platters and her classmates swallowing live rodents, she really wasn't as excited as she'd been the night before to begin this quest.

She spent her morning classes psyching up her courage, determined not to wuss out.

When the bell finally rang for lunch, she lingered long enough to allow the first surge of students out the door. She followed a bit slower, glancing over her shoulder to verify that yes, Ms. Saber had stepped out of the classroom and was watching as Amelia walked to the corner and turned left toward Cafeteria A.

As soon as she turned the corner, she stopped, waited a moment, then peeked back around.

Ms. Saber was gone.

Amelia darted across the hall and hurried after a group of students that were heading in the opposite direction of Cafeteria A.

They turned a corner up ahead and Amelia hurried faster to catch up. She stepped around the corner, then jerked back.

Three of the students had stopped in the middle of the hallway and were talking in frantic whispers.

She couldn't hear what they were saying, but worried they knew she was following them.

She waited a moment, then peeked around the corner again.

The students had started walking and were almost at the end of the hall.

She raced after them.

They took another left. Were they heading back the way they'd come?

But no, up ahead was the school's main staircase. Maybe they'd be going upstairs.

Amelia's heart beat faster at the thought.

She'd never been upstairs because all her classes and Cafeteria A were on the first floor.

The students walked past the staircase and turned left. Again.

Amelia huffed and hurried after them.

What were they doing?

They were walking in circles!

They were now back in the same hallway as Ms. Saber's classroom.

The students turned right and Amelia groaned softly.

Just her luck. She'd followed three students on a circuitous route straight back to her own cafeteria.

Great!

Now what?

Just in case the students were planning to bypass Cafeteria A, she stepped around the corner to check.

Of course not.

Though they weren't exactly going inside the cafeteria, they weren't walking past it either. Instead, they stood outside the cafeteria doors, engaged in what looked to be a heated, though whispered, argument.

Amelia's eyes narrowed. She took a step forward and all three students stopped talking and turned as one unit to stare at her.

All the hairs on the nape of her neck stood on end and for about the millionth time since starting at Shiffer High, she had to clamp down on the sudden urge to flee from her classmates.

One of the students nudged another, who turned and opened the doors and all three disappeared inside the cafeteria.

Fine then. No problem. She still had enough time if she wanted to sneak upstairs on her own.

She turned to head back the way she'd come and jumped as she came face to face with two boys from her English class.

"Hey, Amelia!" Tommy Naked Mole Rat jerked back as he squeaked a greeting.

Amelia never quite knew what to think about Tommy's name. Personally, she would have died every time a teacher called her "Ms. Naked Mole Rat," but it didn't seem to bother Tommy at all, though of course, they called him Mr. In fact, the name kind of suited him, considering his short, tiny frame, which was even smaller than Paulie Porcupine's, and his completely bald head.

"Whatcha doin'?" he asked.

"Uh…"

"Doesn't matter." Eddie Macaw shoved a hand through his bright blue hair, making it stand up even straighter, which Amelia hadn't thought possible. "We're late for lunch."

"Let's go, Amelia," Tommy squeaked, grabbing one arm while Eddie grabbed the other. Together, they pulled her down the hall to Cafeteria A.

"Wait. Is this even your guys' cafeteria?"

It was too late though.

Tommy had already opened the doors, revealing utter chaos inside.

three

foxes

"HAVE YOU GUYS seen Amelia today?" Felicia demanded as she plopped down at the lunch table.

"I don't have any classes with her," Mason said.

"Me neither, but I saw her in the halls before school," Sam said.

"And I saw her in history," Luis said.

"Did she seem all right to you?"

Sam shrugged. "I guess. Why?"

"She just seemed really distracted in art. And the way she looked at me– I'm telling you, she knows!"

Luis groaned. "Not this again."

"Fine, don't believe me! But even if you're right and she doesn't know, it won't be long, not with the way everyone's acting today, treating Amelia like she's crazy or something." Felicia shook her head. "I swear – in art, Kayla Polar was acting like Amelia was the predator and not the other way–"

"Holy scat," someone shrieked, making Felicia jump in fright, scattering precious vegetables everywhere. Before she could get angry though, a scent reached her that made all the hair on her head stand up straight, and deep inside, her bunny froze into stillness.

"Are those–" someone else yelled.

"Foxes!"

Felicia had no idea who shouted that. It seemed like the entire world went mad though. Everyone was scrambling, either for the doors or under the tables.

She just sat there frozen until Luis leapt over the table, grabbed her around the waist and pulled her down into a crouch beside him. "You okay?"

She nodded. It was good to know her brother wasn't a coward *all* the time.

Just when it came to tigers.

She peeked over the table toward the door.

Three foxes stood there, just like she'd scented, looking both terrifying and terrified.

"Why are they here, Luis?"

"I have no idea."

At that moment, two things happened at once.

The doors to the cafeteria banged open and Felicia cringed, worried more foxes were going to enter.

Instead, it was Amelia, looking about as frustrated as she'd ever looked, with Tommy and Eddie at her side. Tommy sometimes ate in Cafeteria A, but Eddie usually preferred to have at least some meat with his vegetables, so it was weird to see him venturing into A. And weirder still to see him with Amelia.

At the same time they appeared in the doorway, Ms. Lioness stormed toward the trio of foxes, a furious look on her face.

Amelia froze in the doorway, uncertain where to look first.

The students all seemed to be in a state of chaos, some of them under the tables, some of them crouched behind them, some huddled against the walls and many, many more appeared to be in a mad dash for the doors at the back of the cafeteria.

Vegetables were everywhere. On the floor, on the tables, in students' hands as if they might somehow be able to wield them like swords to defend themselves against… whatever it was that had them so spooked.

"What are you doing in here?" Ms. Lioness roared as she stormed toward them.

At first Amelia thought she was yelling at them, but then realized the cook's wrath was focused on the three boys Amelia'd been following, who were now cowering against the wall not too far from where Amelia stood.

"You know foxes aren't allowed in A!" Ms. Lioness snarled.

Amelia glanced around the room, confused. What foxes now?

Ms. Lioness came to a stop in front of the boys, hands on hips, and demanded, "Well?"

Amelia edged to the side, the movement catching Ms. Lioness' attention. She whirled, stared at Amelia, Tommy and Eddie for a moment, then drew in a deep breath and said quietly, "I see."

Amelia had no idea what that even meant. What did seeing Amelia, Tommy and Eddie have to do with Ms. Lioness' anger about foxes? And what foxes again?

"You're late, Ms. Finch." Without waiting for a reply, Ms. Lioness transferred her glare to Tommy and Eddie. "As are you two."

"Sorry, Ms. Lioness," Tommy squeaked.

"Yes, so sorry," Eddie said.

"Hmph. Well, hurry up then. Get your lunches and have a seat."

She waited as Amelia, Tommy and Eddie skirted around her and hurried to the salad bar before turning her attention back to the three boys. "You three. Outside. Now."

Amelia let Tommy and Eddie go first, waited to be sure they weren't paying any attention to her, then turned away, hoping to slip back out of the cafeteria.

She'd barely taken a step though, before Felicia was there, latching onto Amelia's arm and turning her back toward the salad bar.

Amelia closed her eyes in frustration, then resolved to try again later. For now, she might as well get some lunch. She quickly worked her way down the salad bar with Felicia bouncing at her side.

"Where have you been?" Felicia asked. "I was worried you were going to miss lunch and I'd have to eat with just the boys for company! Again!"

"Yeah, sorry about that. I was chatting with Tommy and Eddie. Lost track of time." A thought occurred to Amelia and keeping an eye on Felicia out of the corner of her eye, she added, "I didn't realize they ate in the same cafeteria as us."

"Really?" Felicia had a weird look on her face.

"Yeah. I thought for sure they'd head off to a different cafeteria, but we all ended up here."

"Oh, well, I think they usually eat in C." Felicia bounced at her side.

Interesting.

Turning to head to the table, Amelia noticed Eddie and Tommy standing with their trays, looking uncertain about where to sit. "Come on," she said as she walked by. "You can eat with us."

They followed her and Felicia to their table.

As soon as they were seated, Amelia said, "So you guys usually eat in Cafeteria C?"

Eddie froze, a piece of lettuce dangling from his fingers. "Uh. Yeah. Sure."

"Where is C anyway?"

"Upstairs," Tommy squeaked.

"Is it just like this one?"

"Um. I guess. Yeah. Sure." Eddie shoved a couple pieces of lettuce in his mouth.

"What about the boys Ms. Lioness kicked out?"

"The foxes?" Felicia scowled. "They probably eat in D or maybe even–"

"Maybe even what?" And exactly how far up the alphabet did the cafeterias go anyway?

Felicia glared at Luis, who was sitting next to her. "Nothing."

Amelia doubted it was nothing. She eyed Luis who had an entirely too innocent look on his face. "So how many cafeterias are there again?"

Luis shrugged.

"Felicia?"

"Uh, I'm not sure." She glanced wildly at their friends. "Hey, Mason, do you want to go bowling after school?"

"Huh?" Mason looked up from the vegetables he was focused on eating.

"Bowling after school?"

"Sure." He went back to his vegetables.

"Amelia, you want to go?"

"Um, yeah, sure, but–"

"What about you guys? Sam? Luis?" Felicia's voice sounded a little desperate. "Bowling tonight?"

They chorused their agreement as well, then went back to their salads.

"Okay, but how many–"

"We always go bowling after school. Either that or sometimes to a movie," Felicia said to Eddie and Tommy. "Do you two want to join us?"

They both looked surprised.

"Um, sure," Tommy squeaked. "I've never bowled before."

"It's a lot of fun," Felicia said, bouncing in her chair. "What about you, Eddie?"

"Yeah, okay."

"Cool. Meet us in the courtyard after school, okay?"

The boys chorused their agreements and Amelia opened her mouth to *once again* ask about the cafeterias, when the bell rang signaling the end of lunch.

Amelia groaned as everyone surged to their feet, her friends still eating veggies as fast as they could. Usually they were done way before Amelia, so something must have happened before she arrived to put them off their food.

Everyone rushed to the door and Amelia followed, keeping pace with Felicia to try again. "So how many cafeterias are there?"

"What?" Felicia dumped her tray and darted out the door, Amelia fast behind her.

"How many cafeterias?"

"Oh, I don't know. I gotta get to class. See you after school, Amelia." Felicia bounced away, then turned and bouncing backwards, shouted cheerfully, "Bowling!" And then she whipped around and was gone.

Felicia raced around the corner, glanced over her shoulder to be sure Amelia hadn't followed her, then hopped over the "Maintenance Only" chain that stretched across the stairs to the basement. She bounced down them as quickly as possible, then darted around the corner into her engineering classroom.

She stalked up to the the table she shared with Luis, Mason and Sam, plopped down her books and glared at them. "You guys were no help at all!"

"What are you talking about?" Sam asked.

"Amelia was asking all those questions and you guys couldn't even be bothered to distract her!"

"Hey, you're the one concerned about everyone acting all weird around her. Well, you were the one acting weirdest of all!" Luis retorted.

"I was not!"

"You so were!" Mason said. "Pretending you didn't hear her questions, changing the subject, not even finishing your sentences."

"That was Luis' fault! He kicked me, making me think I shouldn't tell Amelia about all the other cafeterias, but then she kept asking and you guys weren't helping!" She whirled on Luis. "If you didn't want me to act all weird, you should have just let me answer her question." Felicia plopped down in her chair and groaned. "I told you she knows. Why else would she be asking all those questions?"

"Because she's curious?" Sam ventured.

"Because everyone acted insane when the foxes came to lunch today?" Mason asked.

"Yeah. And what was up with that?" Felicia asked. "What were they thinking?"

"I heard Amelia was following them," Hannah Rabbit piped up from the next table.

"Really?"

"I heard that too," Davey Rabbit agreed. "She was following them so they led her back to her own cafeteria, but then they felt trapped.

Like they had to go inside."

"I heard she wasn't going to go into A after them, but Eddie and Tommy made her," Mark Rabbit said as he walked by, heading for his table across the room.

"I can't believe we all panicked like that," Sam said in disgust.

"I know," Davey agreed. "We were kind of pathetic."

"Especially if the foxes were only trying to help," Felicia said.

Luis groaned. "We're probably going to have to apologize."

"To the foxes?" Hannah exclaimed in horror.

"All right, class, let's get this show on the road," Mr. Groundhog said from the front of the room. "Who can remind us of one of the golden rules of burrow engineering?"

Amelia decided to interrogate the Hedgehogs in biology.

She asked Tessa first, before class even began, but she just shrugged, which wasn't a big surprise. Even though Alex and Brock were no longer harassing her, Tessa was still pretty grumpy.

Like all the time.

So Amelia decided to sit behind Brock at the front of the classroom.

Usually she sat at the back of the room next to Tessa, but since Tessa wasn't talking, desperate times called for desperate measures.

Alex usually sat on the opposite side of the room from Brock, but when he saw where Amelia was sitting, he made a beeline for them and sat next to Brock.

Once he was there, they both slowly turned to face her, equal looks of worry – and yes, a little bit of fear – on their faces.

Okay, so she hardly ever talked to them, and when she did, she was usually calling them out for their sexist, idiotic behavior, but they only had themselves to blame! And besides, they might be her best chance at getting some information.

"So how many cafeterias are there in this school?" she demanded.

They looked at each other, then back at her.

"Six," Brock said.

Seriously? Six cafeterias? "Are they all being used?"

"Sure," Alex said. "We used to only have three, but then–"

"Then what?"

He looked at Brock, who quickly said, "They got too crowded."

Amelia had to think about that for a minute.

She'd never been to a school that had one lunchtime for the entire school, so she supposed it was possible they'd discovered over time the need for more cafeterias. Still.

Six seemed an awful lot.

Almost like overkill.

It also wasn't very convenient since it was a lot of cafeterias she'd have to find and explore.

"What are you guys talking about?" Tessa usually ignored Brock and Alex as much as possible, so Amelia was kind of shocked when she joined them.

"Cafeterias," Alex said.

Tessa scowled.

"What cafeteria are you guys assigned to?" Amelia asked. "I'm in A."

"Oh, we're in C with Tessa," Brock said.

"But I thought Felicia said Tessa was in A with us." Amelia looked at Tessa. "Not that I've ever seen you there."

Tessa just shrugged.

"Is that where you've been hiding, Tessa?" Brock asked.

"Yeah, because we've looked for you in all your regular hiding places and you're never there anymore," Alex said.

Tessa just grunted.

Unbelievable.

So even though Tessa'd been assigned to C, she was now hiding in A to avoid her stalkers?

Amelia glared at Brock and Alex, who both threw up their hands in surrender.

"Hey, we've been much better lately," Brock said.

"Yeah, we're not following her around or anything," Alex said.

"Right, Tessa?" Brock asked.

Tessa just rolled her eyes and walked away.

Amelia huffed, stood and followed Tessa to the back of the room. She tried to find out whether the boys were harassing her again, but Tessa just grunted that they were fine and didn't speak for the rest of class.

Felicia quivered with excitement as she hurried from the girls' locker room.

It was so hard when she had to wait until science class, much better when they got to shift in engineering. Still, no matter when it happened, or which teacher was in charge, *this* was always the best part of her day.

She hopped across the hallway and entered the quiet, unfinished area of the school's basement.

She inhaled and shivered at the exquisite smell of dirt and roots, plants and dandelions.

It was amazing.

Luis hopped up beside her, rubbing his body against hers and the two of them took off at a run, racing toward the warren they'd been building, Sam, Mason, Hannah and Davey on their heels.

The six of them raced over the top of their warren, kicking dirt this way and that, chasing each other all over the place, darting around mounds of dirt and over the top of them, rejoicing in the glorious feel of earth beneath their feet and the freedom of letting their rabbits out.

"All right. That's enough shenanigans. Listen up!" Mr. Mole called out.

The rabbits all froze in place and turned to face him.

"I want you to take a moment and explore your warrens carefully. The foxes were in here earlier and they modified your warrens for their own purposes. Your job is to sniff out where the foxes have been, how they've changed your warrens and made them unsafe for bunnies and fix them."

Foxes.

This was terrible! Hadn't the foxes caused enough trouble for one day?

"All right." Mr. Mole clapped his hands. "You have thirty minutes to discover the issue and to fix it. Each group will report back to the class exactly what you found and what you did to solve the issue. Go!"

There was a mad rush as rabbits everywhere entered their warrens and started to sniff out the foxes' nefarious deeds.

four

seeking b through f

IN TECHNOLOGY, AMELIA asked Paulie what cafeteria he ate in and he absently replied, "B."

When she asked Katrina, she only got a glare.

"She's in F." Victor leaned forward and Amelia jerked away.

Just in time too as it appeared he'd been about to sniff her hair. Again.

Victor grinned at Amelia. "We're in F together, right, Katrina?" The way he said it sounded somewhat obscene.

Katrina obviously thought so too because she whirled around and let out a very realistic snarl.

Victor jerked back and disappeared behind his computer.

Katrina settled back in her own chair and said, "Why are you so interested in the cafeterias, Amelia?"

It wasn't that Katrina asked – though it was kind of unusual for Katrina to show interest in, well, anything – it was more the way she asked. Almost like she was suspicious.

"No reason. Just curious. I've never been at a school with more than one cafeteria."

"Really-really?" Paulie turned to stare at Amelia. "Where did everyone eat-eat-eat?"

"In the same cafeteria."

"Your schools must have been awfully small," Katrina said.

"No, they just had lots of different lunch times and we'd only get about 25 minutes to eat."

"25 minutes!" Victor leaned forward again. "How could anyone get enough to eat in 25 minutes?"

"Well, actually, once we made it through the cafeteria line and got seated, it was probably more like 15 minutes."

"That's barbaric!" Katrina said.

"How did you keep from starve-starving?" Paulie asked.

Amelia shrugged. "We just ate really fast."

"Must have savaged your digestive system," Victor muttered.

Amelia thought about that word later in calculus when Laney muttered, "Weirdo," as Amelia sat down.

She thought of it when Laney stared at Amelia like she was a freak all through class.

And she thought of it when Laney finally said, "So are you just naturally weird or is it something you have to work at?"

Yep. Savage really was the perfect word. It described exactly what Amelia'd like to do to Laney's attitude.

Instead though, Amelia simply smiled at her and said, "It comes naturally, of course."

Laney rolled her eyes and went back to ignoring Amelia.

Amelia studied her for a moment, then said, "You know, I hardly ever see you at the bowling alley or the movies. You're always welcome to join us, Laney. I hope you know that."

Laney stiffened for a moment, then muttered, "I have to work after school."

"Oh." Amelia made a face. "That sucks."

Laney shrugged and looked like she was about to say something, but the bell rang signaling the end of the school day. She jumped up, grabbed her books, started to walk away, then turned back to mutter, "See you."

"Bye, Laney." Amelia watched her leave, then gathered her own things and walked to her locker, pondering everything she'd discovered that day.

While she hadn't yet figured out where the extra cafeterias were, she *had* discovered there were six of them.

Perhaps more importantly though, she'd had an actual, somewhat civil conversation with Laney Siamese.

It was a miracle!

Amelia shoved her books into her locker, closed the door and jumped as Felicia leapt into her space.

"Bowling!" She bounced up and down, cheering like a maniac.

Amelia laughed. "You're such a nut, Felicia!"

"Really? I like nuts!" She bounced up and down as she spoke. "Are you ready to go?"

"Not yet." Amelia made a split second decision. "I'm going to stick around and work on my art project for a little while."

"But, Amelia! Bowling!"

"I know. I promise I'll be there, I just need a little bit of time, okay?"

"Well, I could stay with you if you want."

"No, no. You go ahead, get everyone set up on the lanes and I'll be there as soon as I can."

"But you're so much better at teaching the rules than me and

Tommy and Eddie haven't ever bowled before!"

"You'll be fine. It'll be good practice for when I'm not around."

Felicia huffed. "Fine. You'll hurry though, right?"

"I promise."

"Okay." Felicia grinned. "See you later!" She bounced away.

As soon as she disappeared around the corner, Amelia headed for the girls' bathroom where she hid in a stall until the sounds from the hallways died down. While she waited, she made a plan. She'd pretty much been everywhere on the first floor, so she figured the other five cafeterias were probably upstairs. She'd search the second floor first, then keep moving upward.

When a couple minutes had passed without hearing any noises from the hallway, Amelia slowly ventured out of the bathroom.

The girls' restroom was right across the hall from Ms. Saber's room and she had two choices for stairs. There was a smaller staircase at the end of the hall that she could use. She'd only have one classroom to get by, but it was Ms. Saber's room. Or she could go the other way and have to sneak past Mr. Sloth's, Ms. Hedgehog's and Ms. Raccoon's rooms.

The truth was, Amelia'd rather be caught by *any* teacher other than Ms. Saber, so three classrooms it was. Turning left, she darted past the hall leading to A, then sneaked past Ms. Hedgehog's and Mr. Sloth's doors. She peeked around the corner, darted past Ms. Raccoon's room and stepped into the stairwell.

She paused to listen. No sounds of anyone walking up or down the stairs.

Dragging in a deep breath, she slowly climbed the stairs to the second floor.

She peeked into the hallway, but then reconsidered.

Maybe she should start at the top, on the fourth floor.

It was the furthest away and therefore might be the hardest to access. In case she never got this chance again, she wanted to take it now.

Turning, she ran up the next two flights of stairs, then stood at the top and listened.

She couldn't hear any voices or footsteps.

She crept to the stairwell's entryway and peeked out. The halls were deserted.

Her heart was pounding.

Why was this so scary?

It was just a school, for heaven's sake!

It *should* be the safest place on earth.

Dragging in a deep breath for courage, Amelia walked to the first classroom she saw. The door was closed and the lights were out. She tried the doorknob, but it was locked.

Great.

This was going to be a very short expedition if she couldn't even get inside any of the classrooms up here.

She headed down the hall, peeked around the corner and saw the next hall was also empty. She checked two more classrooms, but they were both locked as well.

She peeked around the next corner and realized she was standing pretty much at the same spot on the fourth floor that she'd stood at earlier that day on the first. She was staring at a pair of doors that looked suspiciously like the same doors Tommy and Eddie had dragged her through at lunchtime.

Was this one of the extra cafeterias?

Darting down the hall, she grinned at the label to the left of the door.

Cafeteria E.

She grabbed the handle and almost jumped for joy when the door opened silently. She walked inside and the door swung shut behind her. The lights were out, but there were two walls of windows letting in enough natural lighting she could see perfectly.

It looked almost exactly like her own cafeteria. The walls were lined with buffet bars she imagined had been full at lunch earlier that day.

The only difference she could see was that A's kitchen was at the front of the cafeteria, to the left of the doors, but this cafeteria seemed to end where the kitchen would start.

Still, there had to be a kitchen somewhere. Right?

Amelia walked slowly through the tables, making her way to the back of the room.

Still no kitchen.

She made a slow turn, hands on hips, examining each wall carefully. She'd made almost a complete circle before she saw them.

There was a set of swinging doors on the same wall as the doors leading to the hallway. They were set in the corner, almost unnoticeable, to the point that Amelia's eyes had almost skipped right over them.

She hurried to the doors and slowly pushed one open.

Yes!

The kitchen.

She stepped into the dimly lit room filled with stainless steel appliances and countertops.

Amelia huffed.

Everything looked so normal.

There was a door labeled pantry, but it was locked.

She was about to give up when she noticed a second set of swinging doors, on the opposite wall as the ones she'd come through.

She hurried through those and grinned.

She was standing in another cafeteria!

It looked identical to the one she'd just left and honestly to her own cafeteria as well.

Shaking her head, she walked toward the front of the room and pushed open the doors standing there. As she suspected, they led right out into the hallway where she found herself standing directly across from the entrance to cafeteria E.

She turned and examined the doors she'd just exited.

Sure enough.

To the right of the doors was a label that said *Cafeteria F.*

Great.

She'd found two of the mysterious extra cafeterias, and all she'd learned from them was that they were right across the hall from each other and they shared a kitchen.

Otherwise, she'd learned nothing.

It didn't make sense.

Why was everyone so worried about keeping her away from the extra cafeterias?

She sighed and wandered around the rest of the floor.

There were several additional classrooms, but all of them were locked.

She couldn't even tell from the outside what the classrooms were.

She looked inside each one and all she could tell from the small window was that most were perfectly normal. Desks or tables. Chairs. A podium for the teacher.

There were two classrooms with no windows at all, so she had no idea what was inside them.

And three classrooms were full of high tech equipment. Computers. Copiers. Printers.

She could see one of the classrooms had a stack of colorful looking brochures on a table at the front of the room. She wished she could get her hands on one. She bet it would tell her a bunch about the class, but of course, the door was locked.

Feeling like a complete failure, she turned down the final hallway, tried another classroom door (locked again) and started to turn away when she realized what she'd seen. She turned back and stared. There was a spiral staircase in one corner of the classroom that led straight up to the ceiling. She was on the top floor though.

Maybe the staircase was just decoration and led nowhere.

Or maybe it led to the roof.

She really wanted to see where it went, which meant sneaking in when classes were in session since she figured that'd be the only time the door was left unlocked. She shuddered at the thought of being caught sneaking around the school, then figured she could just claim she was lost.

Right.

Three floors above where all her classes were. No one would believe that.

She'd just have to not get caught.

The next classroom wasn't a classroom at all, but a library that she thought was right above where the first floor library was. A closer look through the windows revealed a wide staircase leading down, perhaps to the floor below. No stairs leading up though. She wondered if the stairs leading down meant there was a library below this one and if this was the library she wasn't supposed to see. She tried the door, but it too was locked.

How annoying! This entire floor was a complete bust.

Maybe she'd have better luck on the third floor.

"The bunny-bunnies are going bowling again," Paulie said to Melvin.

Melvin grunted. This wasn't exactly good news. If the bunnies were going, Amelia was likely to be there too. The night before had been a total fluke. And now that he knew how much fun bowling really was, it was even more disappointing that he couldn't join his friends.

"We should go-go."

"Are you crazy?"

"I don't think Amelia-Melia's joining them."

"How do you know that?"

"Because they all just went into, into the bowling alley, and only Jake-Jakers, Katrina-Rina, Tommy and Eddie were with them. Well, and a bunch of bunny kit-kits."

"Tommy Naked Mole Rat?"

"Yep-yep."

"And Eddie Macaw?"

"Yep-yep."

"Huh." Melvin sat up and glanced over at the bowling alley. He'd been spending an awful lot of time on this bench in the town square lately. Just hanging out, watching his friends go into the bowling alley or the movie theater and then sneaking in later to watch the fun from the balconies. He was tired of lurking. "What if she's already there?"

Paulie held up his phone. "I texted Jake-Jakers. She's not coming until later-later."

"All right then." Melvin stood up. "Let's go check it out."

Amelia followed the same path on the third floor as she did on the fourth, but moved faster this time since she knew where she was going.

She found Cafeterias C and D right away. They were set up just like E and F and the pantry was locked in their kitchen too. She was still missing B, but imagined she'd find it on the second floor.

All the classrooms were locked again, though she did find a theater that had stadium seating and a huge stage.

She ran down the stairs toward the stage and exited the theater from a set of doors on the left.

Whoa. She looked back into the theater and realized it spanned two whole floors. She'd entered at the top of the stadium on the third floor and had exited from the bottom onto the second.

She pondered going back up the stairs to finish her exploration of the third floor, but figured she hadn't missed much. A couple more locked classrooms at most, though she was curious to see where the stairs in the library led to. She decided to explore this floor first and go back up if she needed to.

Sadly, the second floor was pretty much a repeat of the ones above. The only difference was this floor had only one cafeteria, like the first floor did, and it was located directly above A. Otherwise, everything was pretty much the same.

Locked pantry in the cafeteria's kitchen.

Locked classrooms.

Locked library. Though this library had a wide staircase leading up to the floor above and another one leading to the floor below. Interestingly, the one leading downward was roped off. Standing there, staring at that roped off staircase, Amelia was pretty certain she knew where it came out.

The library on the first floor, the only one she'd ever been inside, had a staircase leading upward and a rope stretching across it with a sign that said "staff only." Up until now, Amelia hadn't questioned that sign at all. It had seemed perfectly reasonable for a section of the library to be for staff only. She'd figured it housed textbooks and teaching materials.

Now though, on the other side of that staircase, realizing that only the stairs themselves were roped off, preventing travel between the two libraries, Amelia had to wonder. Was *this* the other library no one wanted her to see – a library that spanned three floors?

Amelia couldn't even imagine it. Three floors of books she'd never read, books she was sure would have answers to all her questions.

Amelia wanted access to the library more than ever before.

Which meant she now had to sneak into the classroom with the spiral staircase *and* into one of the libraries, and since everything seemed to be locked after hours, she'd have to do it during the school day with students and teachers everywhere.

Frustrated that she'd only discovered more questions rather than any answers, Amelia raced down the stairs to the first floor, plotting her next steps as she went.

When they walked into the bowling alley, Paulie pointed toward where Jake was playing.

Melvin took one look and said, "No way."

Jake was on a lane with Tommy, Eddie and Sam, which wouldn't be so bad except they were surrounded by girls. Kelly, Rosa and Sally were bowling on one side of their group while Felicia and Tessa were bowling on the other.

Paulie had failed to mention the sheer number of girls in the alley today.

Melvin scanned the lanes, searching for an area that wasn't already guaranteed to bring out his antlers.

Katrina and Mason were bowling at the opposite end of the alley. And between them and all those girls were lanes that were either empty or filled with little kids.

Melvin sniffed.

Bunny kids.

Scented like Jake and Katrina got roped into bringing their bunny siblings. Or maybe Felicia and Luis were. Or Mason. Or Sam.

No such thing as a bunny only child.

Melvin snorted at the thought. "Come on."

Paulie started to follow, then grabbed Melvin's arm and pulled him to a stop. "Wait-wait-wait. Why Katrina-Rina?"

Melvin gave Paulie a look. One that said, "Are you stupid?"

Paulie groaned. "Right-right-right."

After a long day at school trying to control his moose, Melvin just wanted to relax. Which wasn't possible around most girls. "You can go join Jake if you want. I've told you before, Paulie, you don't have to miss out on the fun just because–"

"No way, Melvin-Elvin. We're going bowl-bowling! Two-two-two days in a row-row!"

Melvin grinned. "Well, come on, then." He led the way over to where Katrina and Mason were bowling.

A few minutes later, they'd both been added to the board and a new game was underway.

"That girl is getting entirely too curious."

Amelia froze. She stood at the bottom of the stairs, completely exposed to anyone who walked by. She took a couple steps to the side and flattened herself against the wall. She did *not* want to get caught by Ms. Saber.

"I told my brother this was a terrible idea."

Or Mr. Grizzly.

Great.

The two scariest teachers on campus were right outside the stairwell.

"I thought since Joe was on the Town Council, not to mention Principal Armadillo, they'd be able to talk some sense into those idiots, but apparently that didn't happen," Mr. Grizzly said.

"You know, if it was just George Finch, it wouldn't be such a big deal," Ms. Saber said. "That man's so distracted, he didn't even figure things out at the rescue event."

"Yeah," Mr. Grizzly grunted. "But the girl."

"She's just too smart," Ms. Saber said. "She's in my English class and I swear, she notices everything. Points out things in the books we read I never even noticed. Though that could just be a side effect of her humanity. Still she's going to figure things out."

"As long as she doesn't come near my gym, I can claim a total lack of responsibility."

"Oh, that's just great, Karl, way to care about your fellow–"

The words became fainter and fainter as Ms. Saber and Mr. Grizzly walked away until the last word was so quiet, Amelia didn't hear it at all.

She leaned her head back against the wall and gasped for breath.

That had been entirely too close.

She could barely breathe for the anxiety she was feeling.

She had to get out and off school grounds.

Now.

Thank goodness the school's entrance was only steps away. All she had to do was exit the stairwell and get to the doors.

Maybe a hundred feet. Tops.

Mr. Grizzly's gym was in the opposite direction of the entrance.

But Ms. Saber's classroom.

If she was in the hall.

If she was looking toward the entrance.

She'd see Amelia.

Dragging in a deep breath for courage, Amelia pushed away from the wall, peeked out of the stairwell and looked both ways.

No one.

She crept down the hall, then glanced around the corner toward Ms. Saber's classroom.

No one.

Dragging in a deep breath, she darted across the hall, through the lobby and out the main doors.

Even though Melvin wasn't exactly coordinated, he was actually pretty good at bowling. His moose was really strong so he was able to get some speed and spin to the ball. Of course, Katrina was much better, but he and Mason were pretty evenly matched.

Paulie wasn't bad either. Even though he couldn't get as much speed, he had great aim.

It wasn't until around the eighth or ninth frame that Melvin's inner moose started to get agitated. It was a different sensation than he was used to though. Usually, it would start with a tingling in his forehead and he'd know Sudden Antler Syndrome was imminent.

This time, though, it wasn't really a tingling. It was more the feeling of his moose swelling inside, almost like the entire animal might burst free at any moment.

He looked around wildly, wondering what had his moose so freaked out.

It couldn't be Katrina.

Could it?

His moose had never been interested in impressing Katrina before and his peacock was so intimidated by her, his antlers that were always on the verge of breaking free seemed to actually shrink inside him whenever she was around. He couldn't imagine anything scarier than Katrina, so what on earth could be causing his moose such turmoil?

Paulie must have felt something too because he leaned over and asked, "Is it just my imag-imagination or are Mason and Katrina-Rina totally into each other?"

Melvin groaned.

Of course.

The pheromones of the tiger were riling up his moose!

He eyed Katrina, who bumped her shoulder against Mason's right at that moment.

Melvin shook his head, amazed when the bunny didn't even stumble.

He'd honestly never seen anything so scary as Katrina Tiger flirting with her prey. "Ridiculous."

"That's not a pair-pairing I would have ever-ever predicted," Paulie said.

"Me neither."

By the end of their game, Melvin was desperate to escape before Rampaging Moose Syndrome became something else he had to dread.

"Not yet, not yet, Melvin-Elvin. Just one, just one more!"

Melvin shook his head. There was no way he'd survive another game around that flirty tiger.

"With the bunny-bunnies!" Paulie grabbed his arm and tried to tug him across the room.

Of course, Melvin didn't budge.

"Please, please, Melvin-Elvin. Just one, just one, just one game!"

Melvin groaned. "Fine. But if I antler-up, I'm blaming you."

"Where'd every-everyone go?" Paulie demanded when they reached the bunnies. "Where's Rosa and Sally and Kelly and Tessa? Where's Eddie and Tommy and Jake-Jakers?"

"They went upstairs to work on their homework," Felicia said. "You guys can bowl with us though."

Melvin hesitated, but since he'd managed to control his moose all day, surely he could handle one more hour.

Amelia froze at the top of the stairs outside the school.

Ms. Saber and Mr. Grizzly stood in the parking lot, talking.

Neither was looking her way, but she was out in the open.

If they glanced over, they'd see her.

Heart pounding, Amelia hurried down the front steps and darted to the side. She slipped behind some of the bushes that stood in the shadows of the school and peeked out, just in time to see Ms. Saber grab hold of Mr. Grizzly's shirt, pull him to her and kiss him.

Holy–

Amelia hurtled back into the bushes.

They were in the school parking lot!

Anyone could see them!

She'd seen them!

Now she was scarred for life.

What was it about that parking lot?

First her dad and Debbie!

Now Ms. Saber and Mr. Grizzly!

At least her dad and Debbie hadn't kissed.

Just the thought made her shudder.

Still.

Bad enough she'd seen Ms. Saber kissing Mr. Grizzly!

The sound of a car's engine reached Amelia's ears and she peeked out of the bushes once more.

A car pulled out of a parking space and drove away.

Amelia waited to see if a second car would exit the lot, but nothing happened.

What did that mean?

Had the two of them left together?

Or was one of them was still waiting in the parking lot?

Waiting for Amelia?

"Ms. Finch."

Amelia startled so badly, she almost fell into the bush she'd been peeking around.

She swallowed and looked up. "Principal Armadillo."

five

pheromones

TWO FRAMES INTO their game with the bunnies, Melvin rolled a strike.

All the bunnies cheered, Felicia the loudest of them all, and when Melvin walked by, she bounced straight up in the air and kissed him on the cheek. "Congratulations!"

Melvin blushed, staggered back and his antlers exploded from his head, knocking him on his rump.

The bunny kits in the next lanes laughed, then in a sudden burst of movement, hopped down into their bunny forms and raced over to where Melvin was sprawled across the floor.

They hopped all over his chest and shoulders, sniffing at his antlers.

Luis glowered down at him and Felicia stamped her feet. "Come on, guys! Amelia could get here any minute. Turn back human right now!"

"Sorry, Felicia," Melvin muttered.

She just rolled her eyes and lifted one of the bunnies up by the scruff of his neck. "Turn back right now, Cory," she told him sternly.

One of the bunnies sitting on Melvin's chest leapt off, raced down the approach and hopped right over the foul line.

"No, Becca, no!" Felicia wailed. "Get back here!"

Becca darted down the lane and at the last moment, plopped down on her bottom and slid straight into the pins, knocking a couple over.

Leaping to her feet, she raced back up the lane.

Behind her, machines began to sweep the deck and reset the remaining pins in place.

The bunnies crawling on Melvin all jumped down and raced toward Becca, clearly wanting to join the fun.

"Oh, come on, guys!" Felicia stomped her foot again, then cried out when Cory nipped her finger. "Ow!" She jerked and barely caught him before he hit the floor.

Cory immediately kicked his way free and raced after his siblings.

"Not cool!" She shouted after him.

"Um, when do you think Amelia will be here?" Melvin asked, sitting up. "Because…"

"I don't know!" Felicia pulled out her phone and sent off a quick text. "It could be any minute!"

"What'd you tell her?" Luis asked.

"To text us when she's on her way."

"You need to tell her not to come," Melvin said. "Unless you think we can catch them before she arrives."

"I don't know, but maybe I can get them to shift back," Felicia said.

"At least their clothes aren't shredded," Sam said as he began gathering them up. "We need to get them human and dressed ASAP."

Felicia groaned and pulled out her phone again, sending off one quick text, then another, to Amelia. "Keeping this secret's becoming impossible!"

"Don't kid yourself," Melvin said dryly. "It's always *been* impossible. It's just more noticeable the longer we have to hide who we really are."

Felicia sighed. "I suppose. I just hate lying to Amelia and keeping secrets from her. It's not fair. We're her friends!" She stamped her foot and glared at Melvin. "I think you should just go hang out with her. Let your antlers do their thing and then the secret will be out and we can all relax!"

"What?" Melvin looked horrified. "No way! I thought we all agreed to keep tabs on her, to distract her when we need to and to make sure she never finds out."

"Yeah, but it's too hard and she's our friend, Melvin!"

"Well, you do what you want. Show her your bunny if you like, but no way am I going to be the one responsible for outing shifters."

"But it makes sense for it to be you, Melvin!"

"No way."

"Come on, sis." Luis slung an arm around her shoulders. "Leave Melvin alone and let's go wrangle some bunnies."

"Fine," Felicia huffed, "but you're being a terrible friend, Melvin!"

Amelia hurried toward town, thankful Principal Armadillo had bought her excuse of dropping her textbook into the bushes, but worried because she was way later than she thought she'd be.

Felicia had already texted twice, asking how long Amelia would be, and as she was texting back to say she was on her way, a third one came through.

Text before you come, K

Amelia stopped and stared at her phone. Of course, she'd been about to do that very thing. She'd already typed *on my way*, but now she didn't want to hit send. What was happening at the bowling alley that they'd need a warning before she arrived?

Maybe she was being paranoid, but it seemed awfully suspicious.

She'd just decided to hit send anyway when her phone buzzed again.

We can bowl tomorrow instead. No need to come by.

And then again.

K, see you tomorrow at school!

Amelia glowered at her phone, then shoved it into her pocket and started walking again. She was NOT going to warn Felicia that she was on her way and she was NOT going to skip bowling tonight. Something was going on and she wasn't going to miss it. Whatever it was.

It took forever to round up the bunnies.

They weren't even Felicia's little brothers and sisters, but somehow she was the one who ended up having to do all the work.

Even though Luis had offered to help, he and the other boys were totally useless, laughing at the bunnies' antics. And Katrina was so busy flirting with Mason, Felicia wasn't even sure she'd noticed her siblings had gone furry.

Finally, after Cory slipped through Felicia's hands for the third time, she lost it. "Katrina! Get over here and help me round up these kits! They've all gone mad!"

Katrina whirled around and stared.

Mason, predictably, started laughing.

Boys!

Completely useless.

Katrina rolled her eyes and loped over to where Felicia stood in the middle of lane five, glaring at the pin deck, hands on hips. "What's up?"

"I can't get Cory to come out from there!" Felicia pointed toward the pit Cory had disappeared into a few moments before.

Katrina groaned. "Seriously? What's he doing down there?"

"I don't know. He went rabbit on me."

"What? Why'd you let them go furry in here, Felicia? Amelia could show up any minute!"

"It's not like I let them do anything, Katrina! They have minds of their own, you know."

Katrina groaned. "Fine. I'll see if I can coax him out." She knelt and crawled under the pin mechanism. "There's a lot of equipment back here. Are you sure he came this way?"

"I should probably get going," Melvin said to Paulie.

"But-but why?"

Melvin waved a hand at his antlers. "What if Amelia shows up?"

"Felicia told her not to, not to."

"Yeah, but–"

"Just relax, Melvin-Elvin."

Like that was even possible with his peacock still strutting around because of that kiss – no matter that it was only on the cheek – and with his moose still riled up from the lingering scent of tiger pheromones.

"Hey, Katrina. You need any help?" Mason joined Katrina and Felicia on the lane.

Melvin didn't hear Katrina's response, but he sure scented it.

Or at least his moose did.

He stumbled to his feet, his antlers making him sway and his moose pushing against his skin. "I gotta get out of here," he muttered to Paulie and staggered across the alley toward the door.

"What-what?" Paulie raced after him. "Why, Melvin-Elvin? I thought you were fine-fine around Katrina-Rina."

"Yeah well, apparently not when she's flirting with that rabbit. I gotta go before–"

"But your antler-antlers are already out, Melvin-Elvin."

"Yeah, and my moose is about to join them." He was practically running at that point, desperate to get outside and away from the scent of tiger, desperate to give his moose room to breathe. And possibly room to expand.

He was reaching for the door when he saw her. He dove to the side of the glass window and plastered himself to the wall.

"What's the matter-matter?" Paulie asked.

"Amelia. She's in the Town Square. She's headed this way!" Even though he'd done everything he possibly could to *not* be the person who revealed the existence of shifters to humans, it was going to happen anyway.

He was doomed.

In a panic, Melvin focused, trying desperately to make his antlers shrink, but the entire alley smelled of tiger pheromones and they were just getting stronger.

His moose swelled even more and he groaned. His skin felt too tight for his body.

What was that rabbit doing over there?

Didn't he know that tigers weren't good dates for bunnies?

Katrina loped across the alley, crossing over the gutters from one lane to the next, headed to the far corner. She was pretty sure she'd seen a door there and was hoping it would lead to the area behind the pins where Felicia insisted Cory was.

She was super conscious of Mason hopping over the gutters in her wake.

A few minutes later, she and Mason stared down the long hallway that stretched behind the lanes.

"Whoa," Mason said, eyes wide. "It's crazy back here."

It really was. A narrow walkway stretched before them, with lots of complicated mechanical equipment on the left and a countertop covered in tools along the right.

"I'll never be able to find him in here," Katrina muttered. She turned and hustled Mason back out the door. "I'm going to shift. I'll scent him faster that way." She closed the door in his face then quickly stripped. She set her clothes on the countertop, shifted and padded over to the door to scratch it with her claws.

Mason opened the door and grinned at her. "Lead the way, Madame Tiger."

Katrina rolled her eyes, though she wasn't sure it had the same effect in her tiger form, and headed down the narrow walkway, trying to catch Cory's scent. It wasn't easy because the entire back room smelled strongly of metal and oil. She was starting to get worried when she finally caught a faint hint of his scent on one of the machines to the left. A quick glimpse of the machine's number told her she was standing on the backside of the same lane where Cory had disappeared.

Felicia was right.

Cory *had* come through here, but it was really tight quarters. Katrina couldn't follow his scent between the machines because she wouldn't fit and she couldn't tell if he'd moved on because his scent was so faint, it dissipated into the overwhelming scent of oil when she went even one step beyond the machine.

She chuffed in annoyance.

"Hold on!" Mason slid into a gap between two huge pieces of machinery and hopped up onto a piece of metal to stare down into the guts of the equipment she couldn't access. "This is amazing, Katrina. You should see all this complicated machinery. I can't believe humans created all this!" He threw a wild grin at her over his shoulder. "I never really thought about how the pins get set back up or how the balls return to us, but now that I'm back here, I'm amazed."

Katrina growled at him. Who cared about stupid machinery when Cory was missing?

"Oh, sorry. Right." Mason hopped up onto the narrow ledge that ran along the front of the machine and stepped from it to the ledge in front of the next one. He leaned over and looked, then turned to Katrina. "I don't see him, but I don't think he'd want to hang out around all this machinery. Not in his bunny form anyway. It wouldn't feel safe."

That was a good point. Katrina examined the area in front of her. So if Cory didn't go back into the alley, which Felicia didn't think he had, and if Mason was right and he wouldn't feel safe near the machinery, that pretty much left the countertop and shelves to the right.

Melvin tried to think of where to hide, but he was afraid to move. What if Amelia saw him through the window? What if he lost control of his moose?

"What's she doing?" He hissed at Paulie.

"She's almost, almost here. Talk-talking to herself again. You'd better hide, Melvin-Elvin."

"You need to stop her, distract her, make her go away!"

"Too late, too – nope, nope. False alarm. She went up-upstairs!"

"What?" Melvin pulled away from the wall and peeked out the window.

He didn't see Amelia, so he waited a couple minutes to give her time to climb the stairs before pulling the door open. He stepped out sideways (the only way he'd ever fit through any door when antlered up) and looked up.

The stairwell was empty and the door to the balcony was closed.

A wave of relief so intense barreled over him, he almost fell to his knees. "I'm getting out of here," he told Paulie. "You go warn the others that Amelia's in the balcony!"

six

the balcony

AMELIA BYPASSED THE door to the bowling alley and ran up the outside stairs. She stopped a moment at the top to catch her breath, then quietly opened the door and slipped inside.

It took a moment for her eyes to adjust to the darkened interior. She actually thought this upper balcony space was cooler than the bowling alley below it. It had a short bar with drinks and snacks behind it, several sitting areas and a pinball machine. It was just a really cool hangout space, almost like what she imagined an old-fashioned clubhouse would look like.

She'd taken a couple steps into the room before she realized it was occupied.

Eddie was stretched out on one of the couches, his bright blue hair a brilliant contrast against the neutral fabric.

Tommy was on the opposite couch, his head in the lap of a girl Amelia thought she recognized from school. Though he was entirely bald, the girl was petting his head as if he had a headful of hair.

Two other girls Amelia didn't know were sitting at a table working on something. Homework maybe.

None of them seemed aware that she was there.

Amelia hesitated, then walked across the room as quickly and quietly as possible, headed for the half wall that overlooked the bowling alley below.

Tessa wasn't really hiding. Her hedgehog just liked to burrow, so when she'd seen the wedge of space beneath the pinball machine, which was super close to the half wall that overlooked the bowling alley, she'd barely been able to contain herself.

She'd spent some time studying with Rosa and the others, but when Tommy, Kelly and Eddie had retired to the couches, she'd taken advantage of the opportunity to slip away. She'd been under the pinball machine, curled into a ball, studying her history notes ever since.

She loved it under there. It was dark and shadowed, but it wasn't lonely because the others were nearby. The peace soothed her hedgie to the point of near-happiness, an almost impossible state to achieve when stuck in the throes of quilling.

Movement caught her attention.

Amelia was striding across the room headed right for Tessa.

Or rather, the *wall.*

Tessa was crouched low under the pinball machine so she couldn't see the bowling alley below, but she'd heard Jake cracking his knuckles and muttering about a flea-bitten moose a while back so she imagined Melvin's antlers were probably on display again. And just a few minutes ago, Jake had started chuckling about "those bunnies" so Tessa was pretty sure whatever was happening down below wasn't anything Amelia needed to be seeing.

She glanced around, but quickly realized no one else had even noticed Amelia. How could they miss her? She smelled so overwhelmingly human.

Tessa huffed and shoved aside her history book, then rolled out from under the pinball machine right into Amelia's path.

Amelia was so focused on getting to the wall, she almost ran right into Tessa, who came out of nowhere, literally rolling across the ground in a tight somersault before popping up.

"Whoa!" Amelia jerked back a little.

"Hi, Amelia!" Tessa exclaimed. "When did you get here? Everyone's been waiting forever."

Amelia stared. She'd never seen Tessa so animated. It was like she'd suddenly taken on Felicia's personality. "Um. I just got here."

Eddie and Tommy suddenly appeared on either side of Tessa.

Amelia narrowed her eyes at them. They'd been completely relaxed on the couches, looking like they might not move for days just minutes before. Yet now they were here, alert and blocking Amelia's access to the half-wall. "Hey, guys. I thought you were going to bowl."

"We already bowled," Tommy said. "It was pretty fun, but we have a history test tomorrow, so we decided to come upstairs and study."

Amelia nodded. "Cool."

"What are you doing here?" Eddie asked.

"Oh, um, well–" Amelia glanced around the room, her eyes falling on the pinball machine in the corner. "I just thought I'd play a game of pinball first." She edged her way around Tommy, who looked pretty freaked out, and keeping her eyes on the three of them, backed up a couple steps. "Luis keeps beating us, so I thought I'd practice before going downstairs." She swung around and gasped at the sight of Jake Tiger who stood with his arms crossed, staring at her.

She hadn't seen him at all until just now, even though he was in plain sight, leaning against the half-wall she'd been headed for the entire time. How had she missed him?

She cleared her throat and edged a bit to the right, then slowly walked forward, heading toward the corner furthest from Jake where the pinball machine sat waiting. One more step and she'd have a clear view of the bowling alley below.

Jake knew in that moment that Felicia was right.

The human *did* suspect something.

He wasn't sure she *knew* their secret, the way Felicia claimed, but she was definitely trying to figure it out. She'd clearly come upstairs in the hopes of seeing something she shouldn't in the bowling alley below.

The good news was that Melvin appeared to have gone home and Felicia had managed to get most of the bunnies back in human form and dressed.

Of course, Katrina, Cory and Mason were still in the back room, but Jake figured things could be much worse. If Amelia had arrived just ten minutes before, she would have seen bunnies bowling with their bodies and Melvin sprawled on the floor, antlers on display. So all in all, things weren't going too badly.

He didn't try to stop her as she stepped up to the wall and glanced down into the alley below.

Disappointing.

That was Amelia's first thought when she saw Felicia, Luis and Sam herding their little cousins toward the door. Apparently they'd all finished bowling and were getting ready to go home.

Which was probably why Felicia's texts were so abrupt. She'd been trying to get her cousins rounded up and out the door.

There was nothing crazy going on at all.

Amelia huffed. Now she was back to feeling paranoid, as if she'd just let her imagination get the better of her. Except she hadn't. All those conversations she'd overheard meant something and she was going to figure it out.

"I've never played pinball before," Eddie said from behind her. "Show us how?"

"Oh, yeah, sure." Amelia turned to face the pinball machine and started explaining how it worked.

Mason opened the door and stepped out into the alley. He glanced around and once he was certain Amelia hadn't shown up, he turned and nodded to Katrina.

She padded forward, Cory's bunny form dangling from her mouth.

"No-no-no!" Paulie rushed up to them and hissed, "Amelia-Melia's in the balcony!"

Mason whirled to Katrina, who quickly backed up, disappearing once more into the back room. He rushed after her. "Here. I'll take Cory." He reached down and gently took hold of Cory's body.

Katrina released the scruff of his neck and Mason cuddled him close. "I'll take him out to Felicia. You get changed."

A couple minutes later, Katrina strolled out of the back room.

Mason grinned at her. "That was super close."

"Are you sure Amelia didn't see me?"

"Well, no, but I haven't heard any screams from up above, so I'm guessing we're safe for now."

Katrina nodded. "I should get the kits home. Is Cory–"

"Felicia took him to the bathroom to get changed. Walk you home?"

Katrina smirked at him. "Still not worried you might get tiger-mauled?"

Mason grinned. No way was she discouraging him. Plus he kind of *liked* her tiger. "Maybe I'm counting on it." He winked at her.

She rolled her eyes and brushed past him, headed for the front where her siblings were waiting. "Well, come on then."

seven

running away

AS SOON AS the door to the bowling alley closed behind him, Melvin's moose stopped pushing against his skin and settled down. A couple minutes after that, his antlers shrank back into his head.

Melvin leaned over, braced his hands on his knees and muttered, "Thank the shifter gods." He drew in a couple deep breaths, then straightened and debated what to do next. He could go home, but he kind of wanted to stick around and find out what happened from Paulie, so instead, he made his way back to the Town Square bench that he'd claimed as his own.

Things were pretty quiet for a while, quiet enough that he'd started to doze off when Katrina's voice broke into his slumber. "I thought you went home, Melvin."

Horrified that Katrina had followed him with all her tiger pheromones, Melvin flew up off the bench and launched over it, putting the entire thing between them.

Great! It wasn't just Katrina either. She had that crazy rabbit,

Mason, with her, not to mention about a hundred bunny-kits. Or maybe only ten, but it might as well have been a hundred. As an only moose, Melvin had no idea how the bunnies handled life with so many siblings.

And why were they staring at him like that?

"Sooooo, how's the dewlap hangin', Melvin?" Mason asked dryly.

Before Melvin could even think of an answer, the bunnies all giggled and hopped up onto the bench, where they began to jump up and down, begging him to, "Change again! Change again!"

Katrina laughed. "Aw, come on, guys. Leave poor Melvin alone. We have to get home anyway." She glanced at Melvin. "You gonna stay here?"

"Oh, uh, yeah. I'm waiting for Paulie."

"Cool."

"Catch you later, Melvin." Mason grinned at him while scooping bunnies into his arms and settling them onto the ground. "Let's go, guys."

Melvin shook his head and watched as Mason walked off with Katrina at his side, both of them surrounded by bouncing bunnies. Like he'd said to Paulie, that was one pairing he would never have imagined.

Crazy rabbit.

Amelia decided what she needed was a partner. A partner who would help her figure things out. Someone who wasn't involved in the conspiracy.

Except the only person she was absolutely certain wasn't involved was her dad. And he wouldn't even admit the flavors in the ice cream parlor were weird.

Which left her with only one candidate and he always ran away when he saw her.

Plus he might be involved.

Probably *was* involved.

Since he had an animal's last name just like every other person in this crazy town. Of course, now that she thought about it, Amelia's own last name was Finch, so that probably wasn't the best gauge of whether someone was involved or not.

And of all the people she'd met in this town, Melvin Moose, despite running away practically every time he saw her, and despite his tendency to skinny-dip in inch-deep stream water, acted way less suspicious around her than everyone else.

So when she was headed down from the balcony with the gang and saw Melvin stretched out on a bench in the town square, she didn't hesitate. Tossing a quick goodbye over her shoulder, she raced down the stairs and across the street, making a beeline for Melvin.

"Hey, Melvin!" A quick glance over her shoulder and she knew she'd have to be quick. Felicia, Luis, Sam and Paulie were all standing on the sidewalk outside the bowling alley while Eddie, Tommy, Jake, Kelly, Sally and Rosa stood frozen in a line up the stairs. They were all staring at her and she'd swear they all looked horrified.

Turning around, she was just in time to see Melvin hurtling over the bench.

Damn!

He was going to run again.

She raced around the bench and flung herself in his path, arms spread wide.

"Wait! Melvin, I just want to talk to you! How are you?"

He stumbled to a halt, swayed a moment, then shuffled his feet, arms akimbo, a terribly uncomfortable look on his reddening face. He seriously couldn't look more adorably awkward if he'd tried.

"Um. I'm fine. Fine. Yeah. Um. How are you, Amelia?"

"Great. Great. So I was wondering if you could help me with something."

"Um." He threw a glance over his shoulder.

Was he looking to their friends for help? Honestly, his shyness just made him all the cuter.

"Yeah, yeah, of course." He looked back at Amelia, swallowed, then said, "So what's up?" As he spoke, he took two steps back, still looking like he might flee at any moment.

Amelia hesitated, wondering exactly how to say this, but then decided to just take the plunge.

"Oh, no!" Tessa gasped.

"Is that Melvin?" Eddie's voice sounded strangled, as if he could barely force the words out.

"Great," Jake said. "That moose is one second away from revealing us to the human and we'll all get the blame for this."

"What should we do?" Rosa asked.

"Nothing," Felicia said. "Maybe Melvin can control himself."

"Oh, you're not fooling anyone," Luis said. "You're hoping Melvin *can't* control himself."

"Well, she's my friend, Luis. I want her to know the truth."

"Even if it gets her killed?" Sam asked.

Felicia gasped. "Surely it wouldn't. We'd protect her, right?" She glanced around at her friends.

"Yeah, Felicia," Jake said. "We'd protect her. But who will protect Melvin from the Council?"

They all blanched.

"And the teachers," Sam said.

"We should rescue-rescue-rescue him," Paulie said.

"He's doing okay so far," Sally said.

"Yeah. So far," Tommy said glumly.

Melvin couldn't quite understand what Amelia was saying.

He was completely panicked, trying to stay at least two steps away from her because the closer she got to him, the more his forehead itched and tingled.

He took two more steps back and tried to concentrate.

Wait.

Did she just say something about aliens? He shook his head and then regretted the movement because it made his antlers feel as if they might be shaken loose at any moment.

"So I thought maybe you could help me figure things out. You know prove that something's going on."

"Something's going on?"

"Yeah. Because well. You know."

Melvin wanted to shake his head again, but instead focused on keeping as still as possible and just repeated, "I know?"

"Well, you have noticed how different things are around here, right?"

"Uh, what do you mean?" For shift's sake, where were the bunnies? He threw an alarmed look over his shoulder and glared at their friends. They were all just standing there, right by the bowling alley, frozen in place. Why weren't they helping him?

He bugged his eyes out at them, but not one of them moved. They just stared back at him like they were watching one of Amelia's terrifying movies.

"Well, mostly it's the people," Amelia said. "Okay and the ice cream parlor, but mostly it's the people."

"Wait." Melvin stared at her. "What's wrong with the ice cream parlor?"

Amelia huffed. "Seriously? What *isn't* wrong with it?"

"Well, it has ice cream for one." Really fantastic ice cream. *Willow* ice cream. Melvin glanced over at the parlor. Maybe he'd have to get a scoop before heading home. He bet Paulie would be up for trying a new flavor.

"Yeah, but it's not just the ice cream. Like I said it's the people. Or the aliens. Or whatever."

Wait. Was she calling *them* aliens? Or was she saying aliens had invaded town? Like in that horrifying *Alien* movie.

"Like Katrina," Amelia rambled. "I really like her, but she has tiger eyes and striped hair. And Felicia's always hopping and Paulie's always digging–" she stopped.

Melvin just raised an eyebrow, pretty certain she was just now remembering he and Paulie were best friends.

She cleared her throat. "Anyway, I overheard the Town Council talking and they called me human – actually everyone calls me human – and then they said we might have to pay the price and I don't even want to know what that means, and then I heard Ms. Saber and Mr. Grizzly talking and they said I was going to figure things out, only I don't know what they meant, but Ms. Saber said I was really smart and I'd figure things out soon and–"

"I'll help," Melvin blurted out.

"I-what?"

"I'll help." He'd do just about anything at this point to make her stop, to get away from this conversation. "Just tell me what you want me to do."

"Oh. Um. Okay. So I was thinking. There's this class upstairs on the fourth floor and it has a–"

"Wait, you've been on the fourth floor?"

"Oh, um, yeah. After school. So anyway, I went to the fourth floor, but I couldn't get into the classrooms because they were locked, but one of them has this spiral staircase that leads up and I want to see where it goes."

Melvin knew exactly where it went.

The roof.

He also knew she must be talking about the aerodynamics classroom.

No way could Amelia go in there.

The textbooks alone would give everything away.

"So I'm going to try to sneak in tomorrow during lunch and I wanted to know if you'd go with me, maybe be my lookout."

He stared at her. Holy scat, how did he get into these messes? "Um, yeah, sure. I just, I gotta go though, okay? Gotta get home."

"Oh, okay. But you'll meet me tomorrow during lunch?"

"Um, sure, just um, send me the info, when, where, I'll—I'll be there." As he spoke, he shuffled backwards, planning to make a break for it.

"Wait!" She lunged forward. "I need your phone number."

"Oh, right-right. Um." He pulled out his phone. "Give me your number. I'll text you." He continued backpedaling as they spoke.

Amelia rattled off her number and he quickly typed out a message, hit send, then whirled and ran, shouting over his shoulder, "See you tomorrow!"

Amelia stared as Melvin ran away.

Again.

A couple minutes later, Felicia bounced up. "Hey, Amelia!"

"Where's Melvin-Elvin going, Amelia-Melia?" Paulie asked.

"I think he had to get home."

"I'm going to catch up, catch up. See you later-later!" Paulie ran across the Town Square, calling, "Wait up, wait up, Melvin-Elvin!"

"Why does he always run away from me?" Amelia huffed in exasperation.

"Who? Paulie?" Jake asked.

"No. Melvin."

"Oh, he does that to all the girls," Tommy said. "Though maybe more to you."

"So what were you guys talking about," Felicia asked.

Amelia shrugged. "Just catching up." She really needed to get home, think and make a plan. "I've gotta go. I'll see you guys at school tomorrow, okay?" She hurried away.

Melvin grabbed Paulie as he came around the corner and yanked him into the alley that ran behind the movie theater.

Paulie let out a yelp, then relaxed when he saw Melvin. "What's going on-on-on?"

"Come on!" He hurried down the alley, circling around several of the buildings so that they eventually came back out onto the town square, only this time on the opposite side from the bowling alley. As he walked, he sent an SOS text to all their friends.

"What are we doing, Melvin-Elvin?"

"Getting help." He hurried toward the ice cream parlor.

"Oh, no-no-no-no-no! Not Laney Siamese, Melvin-Elvin. She's no help to anyone!"

Melvin rolled his eyes. "Of course not. We're just going to get ice cream before we meet everyone back at the bowling alley."

eight

partners in crime

"I DON'T LIKE this plan, Eddie," Tommy muttered as they followed Amelia out of English class the next day.

"Not to worry. It's a multi-step plan. If she slips past us, we have plenty of shifters waiting in the wings."

Amelia turned toward Cafeteria A, just like she had the day before, but this time, they weren't fooled.

"Come on!" Eddie hurried forward and with perfect timing, he and Tommy slid into Amelia's path just as she was heading back the way she'd come.

"Hey, Amelia!" Tommy exclaimed. "How's it going?"

Before Amelia could reply, Felicia came flying out of A, bounding down the hall toward them at a pretty decent speed.

For a bunny.

"Amelia! Amelia! Amelia!" With each cry of Amelia's name, Felicia bounced closer until she was right at Amelia's side, jumping up and down in excitement. "Come on, come on, come on! I can't wait to tell you the latest news. Actually, it's so great, you're not even gonna believe it."

"What?"

Felicia latched onto Amelia's arm and dragged her toward A, all the while waving excitedly at Eddie and Tommy while bouncing like the crazy bunny she was. "See you later, guys!"

And they disappeared into A.

Eddie and Tommy looked at each other, then burst out laughing.

"Did you see the look on Amelia's face?" Tommy asked.

"And when she looked back at us right before they went into A." Eddie could barely talk he was laughing so hard.

"That Felicia's something else," Tommy said as they walked away.

"Yeah. She's happy all the time, but man when she ramps up the excitement, wow." Eddie shook his head.

"I didn't know anyone could possibly bounce that high without having a stroke or something from all the blood rushing everywhere," Tommy said.

"So what's going on?" Amelia asked as Felicia dragged her through the salad bar line.

"So, I don't know if you noticed last night, but Mason and Katrina were totally all over each other in the bowling alley," Felicia said.

"Um, really? I didn't even notice they were there."

"Yeah, but you got there so late, they'd already left."

"So what do you mean by all over each other? Like are they dating now?"

"Well, I don't know, but I was thinking maybe you could help me figure that out."

Amelia didn't really like that idea. She already had too much going on, she definitely didn't want to add spying on Katrina Tiger to the mix.

"Help you how?"

"Oh, you know. By torturing Mason."

Amelia stopped and stared at Felicia. "Torture?"

"Well, not real torture. *Fun* torture. We'll gang up on him at lunch. Tease him about Katrina, ask him if he's kissed her yet. If she's shown him–" Felicia stopped, a startled look on her face.

"Shown him what?"

"Oh, you know, her bedroom and stuff."

"Uh-huh. So you want us to try and get Mason to tell us the details of his romance with Katrina."

"Yes!"

"Are you sure there is a romance, Felicia? Because I don't really know if–"

"Oh, trust me. There's something going on." Felicia bounced excitedly. "So are you with me?"

Amelia laughed. "Sure. Let's go torture Mason." Actually this sounded like it could be a lot of fun. And could have the added benefit of taking her mind off the fact that once again, Eddie Macaw and Tommy Naked Mole Rat had prevented her from exploring the school during her lunch break. If she didn't know any better, she'd think those two were following her.

Mason's phone buzzed. He pulled it out and saw Sam and Luis doing the same.

They all had a text from Eddie.

Mission accomplished.

"Well, that's a relief," Luis said.

Mason glanced over at the door, just in time to see Felicia walk in, dragging Amelia in her wake. "Yeah, but Amelia doesn't look too happy."

"Holy binkies, Felicia's out of control," Luis muttered.

"Huh?" Sam asked.

"Look at her."

All three of them turned to watch as Felicia waved her arms around and bounced in a circle around Amelia, talking a mile a minute. They couldn't hear her words, but the tone reached them and it was pretty intensely chipper.

Not to mention, she was jumping so high, both feet were actually leaving the floor with every bounce.

"Wow. What's got her so worked up?" Sam asked.

"Well, we did tell her it was her job to get Amelia into A," Mason said. "I guess she thought extra energy was required for that."

"I have no idea why," Luis said. "Felicia has more energy on a normal day than the entire cheerleading team."

Sam made a face. "Yeah, but Laney's on that team. Those cheerleaders have no bounce at all."

Luis laughed. "Okay. Valid point."

At that moment, both Amelia and Felicia turned and stared toward their table with identical looks of speculation on their faces.

"Oh, great," Luis said. "What's Felicia up to now?"

Mason grinned. He was sure it would be something spectacular, whatever it was, and really, he couldn't wait to find out. Since Felicia enjoyed torturing her brother so much, Mason was sure to be entertained.

"So, Mason," Amelia said as she and Felicia settled at their table.

Mason's grin faded as he got a good look at her face.

"What's going on with you and Katrina?"

Seriously? This was the best that Felicia could come up with?

Sam laughed. "Yeah, Mason. Come on. Inquiring minds want to know. How was your walk home with the tigress?"

Mason groaned. "Come on, guys. We're just friends."

"Just friends, huh?" Felicia smirked. "Friends who hold hands?"

Luis busted out laughing. "Aw, man, you should see your face."

"Knock it off, guys!"

"No, seriously, I think it's great," Amelia said. "Katrina's awesome. You're awesome. So why not be awesome together?"

Mason rolled his eyes. "Thanks, Amelia."

"We just want to know, right, guys?" She looked around the table.

"Absolutely," Felicia said, bouncing in her seat.

"Know what?" Mason exploded.

"Oh, you know, like when we're bowling and you two are on your own lane together. Is it okay for one of us to join you or should we leave you love birds alone?"

"Or if you go upstairs into the balcony to do homework together," Felicia said. "Do we leave you alone or can we join you for some studying?"

"Oh, and what about at the movies?" Luis said.

"Right!" Amelia exclaimed.

"Do you guys want to sit alone so you can cuddle?" Felicia asked.

"Or can we all sit with you?" Sam said.

By this time, Mason was sure his face was beet red, it felt so hot. "You guys suck."

"So how'd it go?" Melvin asked Eddie and Tommy as they joined him and Paulie at their table.

"Not bad," Eddie said and told them about Felicia's energetic kidnapping of Amelia.

Melvin laughed. "Well, we figured it all went pretty well, even after you left, since Amelia texted me to say we had to postpone our plans."

Tommy groaned. "Postpone? Does that mean we're gonna have to do this tomorrow too?"

Melvin shook his head. "No, I have an idea. I'm thinking we should do this after school today. We just have to set up the Aerodynamics classroom so there's nothing there for Amelia to find and of course, we need it to stay unlocked. Is there anything on the roof we need to worry about?"

"Well, just the locker rooms," Eddie said.

"We can say they're for sun-sun-sunbathing," Paulie said.

Tommy stared at him. "How do you bathe in the sun?"

"I don't know. I just heard it's something, something humans do."

"That doesn't sound right," Melvin said. "Are you sure, Paulie?"

"I think so, I think so."

"But no one can bathe in a sun," Tommy said. "Bathing requires water, not sun."

"It means bathe in sunlight," Laney Siamese said as she walked by. "You guys are such morons."

"Hey! What are you even doing in here?" Eddie asked. "You're supposed to be in E."

Laney sniffed over her shoulder at them. "Yes, well, some of us have friends. I'm eating with the team today." And she flounced away.

"I'm eating with the team today," Tommy mocked Laney under his breath.

Melvin snickered. "Well, as annoying as she can be, she's also pretty smart. Bathing in sunlight. It actually makes sense."

"Yeah, well, she's a kit-cat-cat," Paulie said.

"We know she's a cat. What's that got to do with anything?" Eddie asked.

"Cats love the sun-sun-sun."

Melvin laughed. "Well, that's true."

"Yeah," Tommy muttered. "She probably sunbathes half her life away."

Amelia's phone buzzed on her way to biology. It was Melvin.

After school?

She replied, *Doors locked.*

I'll get us in.

Really? Awesome.

They texted a couple more times setting things up and she spent the rest of the afternoon anticipating what she and Melvin might discover after school. She couldn't wait.

Biology was torture (long and boring), technology was weird (Paulie kept asking questions about zombies), and calculus was predictable (Victor Hyena sniffed her hair and Laney Siamese was back to snotty).

Finally, though, the end of the day arrived and Amelia rushed out to hide in the girls' restroom again, once more waiting for everything to quiet down.

Melvin was downstairs on the first floor, hiding in the boys' restroom, planning to meet up with Amelia as soon as he received the go-ahead from Eddie.

Eddie had the most critical job in this mission and the one with the highest likelihood of failure.

Eddie's job was to get into Aerodynamics, hide in the boys' locker room on the roof and wait for Mr. Pterodactyl to leave. He then had to hide all the textbooks and unlock the door so Melvin and Amelia could get inside.

Melvin figured Eddie's plan to enter the classroom right at its most chaotic moment at dismissal wasn't a bad one, but it also wasn't a great one. After all, Mr. Pterodactyl was kind of scary. Not as scary as Ms. Saber, but close. Prehistoric shifters were never the ones you wanted to dewlap around with.

As for the rest of their friends, they were all gathered in the theater on the second and third floors because they figured it was the best place to hide out as a group. They should have just left since they weren't required for this mission, but none of them wanted to leave the school before Amelia.

Melvin thought they were being stubborn and stupid, considering the more people hanging around after school, the greater their chance of discovery, but no one listened to him.

He also hated the fact that he was Amelia's partner in crime. How was it that she'd chosen him? Of all the people in this school, why would she choose the one person who was pretty much guaranteed to give away their secret in her presence? He had to be the unluckiest son of a shifter on earth.

When the doors to the theater swung open, everyone hit the floor.

Felicia held her breath until she heard Eddie whisper, "Hey. You guys in here?"

She jumped up and hurried over to Eddie. "Did it work?"

"Coast is clear. Door's unlocked. I texted Melvin. They should be on their way."

"Hurray!" She bounced up and down, then glanced at everyone else. "Why are you guys looking so glum?"

"Do you really think Melvin's going to be able to control his antlers?" Katrina demanded.

Felicia shrugged. "Maybe. He's been getting better at it. I mean, he was fine at the bowling alley the other night. And last night too."

"Yeah, until you kissed him," Luis said.

"Well, I don't think Amelia's going to kiss Melvin." Felicia glared at her brother, hands on hips.

"I didn't think you were gonna kiss him either, but you did," Luis said.

"Wait, how did I miss this?" Mason asked. "You kissed Melvin?"

"It was just on the cheek," Felicia said. "I was congratulating him!"

"For what?" Tommy asked.

Eddie grinned. "Yeah. Share so we know what we've gotta do."

Felicia could feel blood rushing into her face. They were ganging up on her! She glared at Luis. This was all his fault! "He rolled a strike!"

"I've rolled plenty of strikes," Mason said. "You've never kissed me."

"Or me." Katrina grinned and wagged her eyebrows at Felicia, which was really annoying because it made Felicia laugh when what she really wanted to do was kick Mason.

"Good point," Mason said to Katrina. "Actually your brother's rolled a lot of strikes too, but she's never kissed Jake either."

"Stop it!" Felicia stamped her foot. "You stop it right now, Mason Rabbit!"

Everyone laughed, which was also kind of annoying because it made her laugh too.

nine

the roof

AMELIA FOLLOWED MELVIN up the stairs to the fourth floor. He'd insisted on going first, to scope things out and give her a chance to run if she needed to.

She smiled to herself as she climbed the stairs behind him.

He was just so nice.

And cute.

Nice and cute.

He'd blushed the entire time he'd talked to her, then hurried up ahead, checking around every corner, racing up the next flight, then motioning her on up. He always stayed several feet ahead of her, which was also cute.

She wasn't sure if he was doing it to really scope things out or if he was just trying to avoid her like he always did.

Either way though.

It was completely adorable.

They finally arrived at the fourth floor and much to her excitement, the classroom door was unlocked.

"How'd you manage that?" she whispered.

He shrugged. "Come on." He led the way to the spiral staircase and started up it.

Amelia drew in a deep breath and followed.

When she reached the top of the stairs, she glanced around and at first was super disappointed. They were in a small room. A really small room. Like closet-sized.

Then she saw the doors. There were two. One to the left and one straight ahead.

Her heart pounded as she opened the one in front of her. It led out onto the roof.

Which was absolutely huge.

"Wow."

She turned and stepping past Melvin, pushed open the other door. She expected it to open onto the roof as well, but instead, it led to a short hallway. The wall to the right looked like a giant garage door and the wall to the left had two doors, one labeled "girls" and the other "boys."

"Restrooms? On the roof?" She hurried to the girl's door and shoved it open. "Why are there lockers up here?" She wandered further in and stared. "And showers?" Really weird showers. One showerhead was so close to the ground, it might as well be for a mouse. Or maybe people's feet. Another was so tall, it almost touched the roof.

Bizarre.

Melvin cleared his throat behind her. "Um, I heard the teachers sometimes come up on the roof. Maybe they sunbathe up here?"

Amelia turned and stared at him. She suddenly had a horrible vision of all their teachers on the roof in their swimsuits stretched out on beach towels during lunchtime. She shuddered.

"You want to check out the roof?"

"Yeah. Definitely." She hurried past Melvin, exited the locker room and headed for the door to the roof. "I bet we can see the whole town from up here!"

Melvin blanched at those words. He hadn't even thought of that. He hurried after Amelia, wondering if he could convince her to go back inside.

He got about five feet from the door and froze.

Holy scat, they were up high.

So dewlappin' high.

This was not good.

His moose did not like this turn of events at all and neither did his peacock.

His peacock might have wings, but it still didn't want to try flying from this height. And seeing as he couldn't shift into his peacock anyway, but instead was stuck with his moose, he had no chance at all. If he shifted up here, even partially, he was doomed. His moose was so clumsy, he'd fall off the roof in a heartbeat. Antlers first.

He needed to get out of there!

He was turning around when Amelia said, "What the helvetica? Not again!"

Worried she was seeing something she shouldn't, he turned and inched closer to where she stood. "What's up?"

"Those two!" She pointed toward the field far below where two figures were walking.

Melvin squinted. "Is that–"

"Yes. Yes, it is."

"Ms. Saber?"

"Yes."

"And–"

"Mr. Grizzly, yep."

"Am I imagining things or are they–"

"Holding hands? Oh, yeah. But that's not as bad as what I saw them doing yesterday."

Melvin stepped back. He wasn't sure he wanted to know. "What'd you see?" He couldn't believe he'd asked. He really, really didn't want to know.

"They were kissing!"

"What? No."

"Yes! Right over there!" She swung out an arm and pointed. "It was after school. I guess they were leaving. Together. Because only one car drove away."

Melvin gagged. "Seriously, Amelia? Why'd you have to tell me that?"

She shrugged. "If I have to suffer knowing that two of our teachers are getting it on, you're just gonna have to suffer with me."

Melvin shook his head. "That – that's just cruel."

"Yes. Yes it is. Look. They're going into the gym. I don't even want to think about what they're going to be doing in there."

"Stop it! There's no way they're doing anything. This is school grounds. He's the P.E. teacher. She's probably just helping him get ready for class."

Amelia smirked. "Yeah. Sure. Helping him organize his balls."

Melvin groaned. "Come on. Stop!"

She threw a grin over her shoulder at him. "Sorry. I couldn't help it. You're just too easy, Melvin."

He shook his head. "You're a nut. We should get out of here, don't you think? I mean, I sure don't want to be caught by those two."

Amelia sighed. "Yeah. I guess. I'm just disappointed. I mean, I was sure I'd find something. It's super weird there are stairs to the roof inside a classroom, don't you think? I mean, who wants a student coming up here, risking them falling off the roof? There's not even a railing around the edges."

"Yeah, I know." Melvin backed away further. "I think that's why we should go now. I really don't like heights."

Amelia didn't reply.

"Amelia?"

"Shiiiiiiiitake mushrooms," she whispered.

"Hey, you okay?" He stepped forward to see what had her so riveted and closed his eyes in horror.

Everyone's cell phones went off at the same time.

Felicia got hers out first.

Melvin's text was simple.

SOS SOS SOS

And then another arrived.

It's not my fault.

And then another.

#scarred4life

And then one more.

And not because she knows.

At that point everyone was running.

They raced up the stadium stairs, out the theater onto the third floor, down the hall, around the corner and up another flight of stairs.

They burst out onto the fourth floor in one giant mob, then turned as one and raced for the aerodynamics classroom.

Jake reached the door first. He placed his hand over the jam and turned to face everyone. "Calm down." His tiger was in his voice and his eyes were wild.

Felicia gasped for breath and nodded. He was right. They needed to calm down. Calm down.

"They're on the roof. We don't want to startle them."

Eddie pushed his way to the front. "There's no safety rail up there. So everyone be careful. Stay away from the edges and *don't scare the human*."

Jake nodded, took a deep breath and pulled the door open. He led the way to the stairs, but then gestured for Eddie to go first.

Jake followed and Felicia went next. She glanced behind her and saw Luis was at her back.

He nodded encouragingly and she continued to climb.

She didn't like this.

She really, really, really didn't like going up onto the roof of the school.

Her bunny didn't like heights at all.

Stairs were scary, but rooftops.

Bunnies didn't belong on rooftops.

But Amelia was up there.

Maybe discovering the truth about them.

Felicia needed to be there for her friend.

She continued to climb, then followed Eddie and Jake out a door onto the roof.

Melvin stood a couple steps behind Amelia, who stood way closer to the edge than Felicia wanted her to be.

Melvin threw a panicked look over his shoulder, then relaxed when he saw the rest of them filing out onto the roof at his back.

He nodded and turned back to Amelia. "Hey, Amelia, can you step away from the edge please? We'll explain everything, just step back a couple steps, okay?"

Amelia heard Melvin's voice from a distance, but she was too caught up in staring down at the giant grizzly bear with a freaking saber-toothed tiger at his side.

They'd exited the gym not too long after they'd gone in. Only this time, they'd come out a different door.

In different forms.

She couldn't really see the door from this angle, but she imagined it had to be much bigger than the one she'd used the day of the assembly.

The grizzly and tiger were walking together, their sides brushing, then the tiger took off running and the grizzly thundered after her. A moment later, the tiger whirled on the grizzly who rubbed his head against hers, then turned and ran. This time, she chased him.

As Amelia watched their antics, everything started to fall into place. Ms. Saber turned into a saber-toothed tiger. Mr. Grizzly a grizzly bear.

"Amelia?"

"Hey, Felicia." Amelia glanced over her shoulder and saw that her party of two with Melvin had grown significantly.

Everyone was looking at her, concerned expressions on their faces.

Felicia, Luis, Sam, Mason – all rabbits. She turned back to the grizzly and tiger, and staring at them blindly, thought about that for a moment, then moved on.

Tessa, a hedgehog.

Katrina and Jake, tigers.

Eddie, a macaw.

Tommy, an actual naked mole rat.

Naked.

Mr. Grizzly had told him to get naked on Amelia's first day. He'd probably meant for him to turn into his animal, not actually get naked.

Who else?

Paulie, a porcupine.

Melvin. A moose?

"I'm not a real finch, you know. I'm just human."

"We know, Amelia. We like that about you," Felicia said.

"Am I the only human here at school?"

"You and your dad are pretty much the only humans in town," Melvin said.

Amelia nodded.

So, that was a yes.

Melvin, a moose.

Who else?

The teachers.

Mr. Sloth.

Amelia grinned, remembering his slow movements and speech.

Ms. Hedgehog and Mr. Fox.

Mr. Fox's anger that first day, how annoyed he'd been, was even scarier now that she knew he housed a real bonafide fox inside him. No wonder Paulie had told her to stop staring.

Then she remembered Ms. Lioness yelling about foxes not being allowed in Cafeteria A. So those kids were probably actual foxes.

She thought about that for a moment, then moved on.

Ms. Raccoon.

Ms. Spider.

Amelia shuddered, horrified because she really liked Ms. Spider, but wasn't exactly fond of spiders themselves.

Thinking of Ms. Spider made her think of art class. "Wait. Does this mean I really *did* see a tiger on school grounds?"

"Yeah, sorry about that," Katrina said. "That was me."

"And the rabbits?"

Sam cleared his throat. "Me and Luis."

"I knew I wasn't crazy." She'd been in art when she'd seen them, a tiger with a rabbit on its back and another one on its tail. Now that she knew it hadn't been a hallucination, she was rather amazed at the rabbits' courage.

"And you guys survived?" She glanced at the two of them.

Luis laughed. "Aw, Katrina wouldn't hurt us. We're cousins."

Uh-huh. Because cousins were always terrified of each other.

Of course, now that Amelia knew Felicia had a bunny inside while Katrina had a tiger, Amelia was beginning to understand the dynamics a little better.

Below them on the field, the grizzly and tiger had stopped playing and were now stretched out side by side, the saber-toothed tiger nuzzling the bear affectionately. "How does she keep from stabbing him with her giant fangs?"

"What?" Felicia asked.

"Ms. Saber. She's down there cuddling with Mr. Grizzly." Amelia waved an arm.

"Are you serious?"

Eddie stepped up beside Amelia and barked out a laugh. "Oh, now, that's just wrong."

"You think that's wrong."Amelia turned and stared at him. "I saw them kissing in the parking lot yesterday!"

Everyone groaned.

"Say it isn't true," Sam said.

"That's disgusting," Felicia cried. "Are you sure?"

"I promise," Amelia said. "And look at them now. There's no way those two aren't going home together at night."

Everyone groaned again.

Amelia swung around and grinned at them. "You know, I really didn't expect this. I'm actually kind of annoyed about it. I was sure you guys were all aliens."

"Aliens!" Felicia exclaimed. "Like in that horrible movie *Alien?*"

Amelia laughed. "No. Of course not. I thought you were good aliens."

"Like in *Independence Day?*" Tessa asked.

"Those aliens were bad too, Tessa!" Felicia said. "All the aliens are bad!"

"Not all of them," Amelia said.

"Really? Tell me one alien movie where the aliens are good."

"*E.T.*, *Star Wars*, *Star Trek*, *Howard the Duck*, *Guardians of the Galaxy*–"

"Okay, okay. Fine. But guess what?"

"What?"

"We're not aliens!" Felicia bounced with each word.

Amelia laughed. "Yeah. I kind of figured that out. Shapeshifters, huh?"

"Just shifters," Jake said.

Amelia nodded. "Very cool." Maybe not as cool as aliens, but way better than vampires.

"You know what the best part about this is?" Melvin asked.

"What's that?"

"We can all honestly say the *teachers* are the ones responsible for Amelia finally learning the truth."

Jake laughed and clapped a hand on Melvin's back. "Feels good, buddy, doesn't it?"

Melvin nodded. "Feels great."

"I bet it'd feel even better if we could tell them they were responsible," Tommy said.

"Yeah, we really need to pretend you don't know, Amelia," Felicia said. "I'm not sure how the adults would react if they knew."

Amelia shrugged. "That's fine."

"You know what sucks about that?" Melvin asked.

"What-what?" Paulie asked.

"If one of us accidentally lets something slip, the adults will all think we're the ones who revealed shifters to Amelia, even though they did it first."

"No worries." Eddie held up his phone. "I have video *and* photographic evidence should it ever become necessary."

"Ah, good man, good man," Jake said.

Everyone laughed.

"So, um, can we leave the roof now, Amelia?" Felicia bounced the tiniest hop Amelia'd ever seen her make. "I really, really want to hug you, but my bunny's terrified right now. She doesn't like heights."

As everyone started filtering back into the building and down the stairs, Melvin stared at Amelia.

She was laughing and joking with Eddie and Katrina and didn't seem at all fazed by what she'd just learned.

He was so busy watching her, he didn't register that she was getting closer until she stood right in front of him.

"So now that I know your secret, are you gonna stop running away every time you see me?"

"Um, well, see." Melvin shuffled his feet as he hemmed and hawed. He really didn't know what to tell her. So far, she was the only one at school who didn't know about his antler problem and he'd really like to keep it that way.

At that moment the wind shifted, bringing with it the rich and intoxicating scent Melvin associated with Amelia.

He staggered back.

He really needed to get out of there.

Before he ended up stuck on that circular staircase.

"I'll do my best," he said, gritting his teeth and shoving his antlers down as far as he could while backpedaling as quickly as possible.

"Yeah?" Amelia raised an eyebrow.

He knew what she was thinking. He was already breaking that promise.

"Yeah. Just, you know. Later. Okay, bye, Amelia!"

He whirled around and bolted.

Don't forget to turn the page for your bonus story:

Episode 4.5

The Trouble with Pets

The Trouble With Pets (a.k.a. The Great Shifter Rescue)

Shifter High: Season 1, Episode 4,5

Written By

A.J. CULEY

CONTENTS

for all the homeless animals of the world
and the many volunteers
who rescue them

“Wait.
Why do animals need rescuing again?”
– Maggie Fox

“What about bears?
Are there any bears up for adoption?”
– Joe Grizzly

“There isn’t enough bamboo in the world
to make up for this job!”
– Debbie Panda

one

the request

Town Council Meeting

David Peacock was the mayor of Shifterville and, as such, considered himself to be rather intelligent. How then had he gotten himself into this predicament?

"What are we going to do about George?" Maggie Fox demanded again.

Groans resounded around the table.

"I can't keep putting him off. We have to give him an answer."

The entire situation was a farce. When the council had agreed to allow two humans to move to town, David had been sure the teenaged daughter, Amelia, would be the one to look out for. Instead, her father, George, was becoming the real issue.

"It's not just you, Maggie," Joe Grizzly said. "He cornered me at the market last week, demanding to know when we would allow him to hold his adoption event."

"I don't even understand what that means," Steve Armadillo complained. "Who are we supposed to adopt again?"

"Animals, I think," Jessica Canary said.

"But why? We *are* animals!" Maggie rolled her eyes.

"Well, George doesn't know that, now does he?" It still filled David with humiliation to remember that crazy interview with George, back when David thought he'd been interviewing a shifter. It wasn't his fault! With a last name like Finch, he'd certainly expected George to be able to sprout a feather or two, at least on occasion. By the time David had realized George was human, David had been set on this man as their new vet.

George had all the knowledge they'd needed. The man loved animals, had studied all kinds, from the smallest to the largest, both exotic and domestic breeds. Filled with an endless array of knowledge of animal diseases and healthy practices, he'd seemed perfect for their town.

"He's going to be here any minute," Maggie said. "What are we going to tell him?"

"I get the feeling if we say no, we may lose ourselves a vet," David said.

"What?" Steve exclaimed. "After everything we've done at the high school to make it human-friendly, after all the changes the town has gone through to hide our shifter natures, there's no way we're losing our vet."

A knock sounded at the door before anyone could reply and five minutes later, George Finch stood at the front of the table, rambling on about the importance of animals and the duty of humans to rescue them.

David was so confused. He didn't understand why humans were adopting animals in the first place. Didn't they have babies to take care of?

Then Steve said what David was thinking. "I just don't get it."

"It's a rescue event," George said. "What's not to get?"

"I still don't understand why the animals need rescuing," Maggie said. "Rescuing from what?"

"From homelessness. There are a lot of homeless animals in the world. Don't you want to save some of them? This is an animal sanctuary, for heaven's sake! I thought that was the whole point of this town. I just want to host a rescue event so people in the community can visit the animals and—"

"And what?" Joseph Grizzly asked.

"And maybe adopt one or two."

"Adopt who?" Jessica Canary asked.

"The animals!"

"What kind of animals are we talking about here?" Steve Armadillo asked. "Zebras, hyenas, gorillas?"

"Elephants?" Maggie exclaimed. "Because an elephant would be cool."

"No elephants. No zebras. No wild animals. Domesticated, people. I'm talking about domesticated animals who can't survive on their own. Animals who depend on humans to care for them."

"I still don't understand," Steve said.

"Cats. Dogs. Rabbits. Chinchillas. You know. Domesticated pets."

"Pets?" Maggie sounded horrified, and the look on her face was one of complete revulsion.

David knew exactly what she was thinking. Did humans really–

"Animals shouldn't be kept as pets!"

"You do realize I'm a vet," George said. "I have a houseful and a clinic full of pets in dire need of adoption."

"Where did all these pets come from?"

"Everywhere. Every time I leave town, it seems I find some poor stray wandering a parking lot or along the side of the highway. These animals need help. I'm a vet. I can't just ignore the plight of an animal in need. I suppose I could have taken them to a local pound, but—"

"But what?" Maggie asked.

"Not all are no-kill shelters. And the ones that are don't usually have space. Besides I hate seeing the animals trapped in a cage. At least at my house or in the clinic, they have room to roam."

"What does that mean?" Jessica asked. "No-kill shelter?"

George sighed. "It means if the animals aren't adopted right away, the shelter will continue to feed and house them until they are. Of course, by house I mean keep them in a cage."

"What if it's not a no-kill shelter?"

"After a certain amount of time, usually thirty days, the animals will be euthanized."

Jessica gasped.

"That's terrible," Maggie said.

"It's just the way things are done. I love animals, you know I do, but I can't keep them all. Guys, I have seven cats and three litters of kittens that are going to turn into full-grown cats in no time. I have nine puppies and four dogs. I've got three rabbits, a guinea pig, two chinchillas and a ferret. And that doesn't include the animals I'm not putting up for adoption, because they're mine and Amelia's. We need help."

"All right, George. Wait outside for us, will you?" David watched until the door closed behind George and then turned to face the other council members. "Okay. What do we do?"

Jessica made a sound of exasperation.

Steve banged his head down on the table and groaned.

Joe growled, a constant rumble in his throat, the grizzly peeking from his eyes.

David assumed it was because Joe was imagining all those animals being killed simply because they had no home.

Maggie said what they were all thinking. “I guess we’re hosting a rescue event.”

two

shoots

As if her job wasn't hard enough!

Debbie Panda stabbed the END button on her phone and jerked open her desk drawer. She grabbed a handful of bamboo from her stash and started chewing. What was the Town Council thinking?

She already struggled on a daily basis to keep George from discovering the truth about all the so-called animals he treated at their clinic. She grabbed a second handful of bamboo and kept chewing. As if that weren't difficult enough, the Town Council had just informed her she was to help arrange a rescue event for a bunch of *real* animals. She went for a third handful and realized there were only scraps left in her stash. She huffed and slammed the drawer shut.

She rolled herself back from the counter and ripped free a stalk of bamboo from the plant in the corner. It would mean even more interactions between George and the town's shifters, interactions she'd have to somehow monitor—she ripped another stalk free—all at an event held outside the clinic. She chomped furiously on the bamboo.

Didn't the Council realize this was just going to provide more opportunities for George to somehow stumble on the truth? She grabbed the rest of the plant and jerked, ripping the last of the stalks free from the planter. This was going to be a total disaster!

She rolled back to the counter, chewing furiously.

The door to the clinic swung open, and George stepped inside.

Debbie dropped her hand and quickly swallowed her last bite. She still clutched the remnants of several shoots. Her mouth watered just thinking of them. Did she dare continue eating? George rarely even looked at her. Probably he wouldn't even notice if she finished her little snack.

Except he was headed right for her.

George was a tall man, with enough bird-like features, Debbie totally understood why the mayor had believed the man was a shifter at first. With that beak-like nose and hair that naturally fell in layers of grays and browns, almost giving the impression of wings, it was truly amazing he had no animal inside.

Debbie wondered occasionally if way back in his bloodline there was a finch shifter or two. Doubtful, because the ability to shift rarely disappeared from a family's bloodline, even if mixed with humans, simply because the shifter genes were so strong. Still it was an interesting theory to imagine.

"Great news, Debbie," George announced as he crossed the lobby toward her. His brown eyes were shining with excitement and perhaps for the first time since they'd begun working together, he actually seemed to be looking at her as he spoke. Usually, his attention was on a client's folder or in a book or on one of the animals themselves. At that moment, however, his entire focus was inconveniently on her.

"They agreed?" Debbie forced a smile as she stood, hiding her bamboo-filled hand behind her back.

George came around the counter and, in a shocking move, scooped her up and swung her around in a massive bear hug, causing her to drop several of her precious bamboo shoots.

She was a generously shaped, 200-pound woman who occasionally shifted into a panda, and this human just lifted her from the ground like she weighed nothing.

"Put me down, you crazy man!"

George laughed, set her on her feet and beamed down at her. "This is going to be great, Debbie! The Town Council agreed. They're even going to let us host the event at Town Hall. It's a great location, lots of space for us to set up pens for the animals and for people to interact with them. Amelia will be so excited."

Debbie raised an eyebrow at that. Amelia was pretty attached to all the animals her dad had rescued, so Debbie wasn't sure the teen would be all that excited to see them go.

As if thinking of Amelia had produced her, the door swung open again and there she was, with her bunny shifter friends at her side.

"Hi, guys." Debbie stepped away from George, who was still standing ridiculously close. As she moved away, she noticed a couple of her shoots lying on her desk. She quickly snatched them up and had her hand halfway to her mouth before she realized what she was doing. She forced herself to open her desk drawer and drop the shoots into its depths. She'd finish them off later. "How was school?"

"Super awesome!" Felicia Rabbit bounced to the counter, full of hoppy energy as usual.

Luis rolled his eyes and followed his sister at a slower rate. "We're headed to the bowling alley but thought we'd stop and see how the animals are doing first, right, Amelia?"

Amelia didn't answer. She stood just inside the door and stared at her dad and Debbie, a look of suspicion on her face. "What's going on?"

Great. The kids were going to think something was brewing between Debbie and the human. Not that she'd mind if that were the case. His absent-minded humanity was actually kind of adorable. Plus he was shifter-strong. She eyed George, noticing for the first time the muscles packed along his beanpole frame.

"Best news ever, Amelia!" George bolted around the counter and flung an arm around his daughter, hauling her close. "The Town Council finally agreed to the rescue event."

"Oh."

Just as Debbie had expected, Amelia didn't look as thrilled as her father was.

"What's wrong, sweetheart? Aren't you happy for the animals?"

"Of course, I am, Dad. I just . . . you know." Amelia shrugged. "I'll miss them. We're not letting just anyone adopt them, right?"

"Of course not! We'll set up some rules, educate people about the animals, make sure they're really prepared."

"And make home visits?"

Home visits? What did that mean?

"I suppose, if that's what you really want."

"I do. We have to make sure the animals go to good homes."

Shoots and leaves! Was she talking about visiting shifter homes? Debbie glanced at the bunnies and saw they looked as worried as she was. "I don't think that's a good idea."

"What? Why?" Amelia glared at her.

Debbie didn't know what to say. She couldn't tell them the truth: that they might see things they shouldn't.

"It implies a lack of trust," Luis said.

"Yes, that's it." Debbie was impressed. The kid thought fast on his feet.

"Hmm. They're right, Amelia. I mean, this is a pretty small town, all things considered. We don't want to upset our neighbors."

"But, Dad—"

"How about if we request references instead?"

"How will we know the references are trustworthy?"

Debbie rolled her eyes.

"Oh, come on, Amelia." Felicia bounced back to her side. "All you'll have to do is ask around. People in this town love animals. No one's going to risk having an animal go somewhere they won't be safe."

Amelia hesitated. "Fine," she finally said. "At least three references though, okay, Dad?"

"You got it, sweetheart."

"Do you need help with the animals today, Dr. Finch?" Luis asked.

"Naw, we've got it all taken care of. You kids go have fun." George grabbed a folder from Debbie's outbox, opened it and wandered away.

Debbie knew by the time he'd taken three steps, he'd already forgotten the teens in the lobby and her too. He was lost in his own world again.

It really was kind of cute, the way he—

"What about you, Debbie?" Amelia asked. "Do you need any help?"

Debbie jumped and looked away from George's retreating form.

Amelia stood right at the counter and was glaring at Debbie suspiciously.

She let out a nervous chuckle before quickly assuring the kids she had everything in hand.

Five minutes later, the door swung closed behind them, but not before Amelia cast one last scowl over her shoulder.

Holy shoots, that girl was suspicious!

And speaking of shoots…

Debbie opened her desk drawer and grabbed the last of them, thrilled to finally be able to finish her snack in peace.

three

the bamboo killer

"DID YOU SEE The Ogle Meister making eyes at my dad?" Amelia demanded the second the door closed behind them.

Felicia, who'd been happily bouncing at Amelia's side, froze mid-bounce. "What do you mean?" She lowered her heels and stared at Amelia.

"Don't tell me you didn't notice how close she was standing to him when we walked in!" Amelia wasn't sure why it annoyed her so much, just that he was her dad and… Gross. She didn't want to ever think about him and romance.

Besides, she was pretty sure Debbie was after something. Nobody had ever shown any interest in her dad before. Like ever. Or if they did, the minute his lack of attention toward them was apparent, their interest died. No woman wanted to be an afterthought to her guy. So why was Debbie all of a sudden staring at her dad with that look on her face?

"Are you talking about Debbie?" Luis asked.

"Yes, of course, Debbie! Who else would I mean?"

"But Debbie's nice," Felicia protested.

Amelia huffed. "Well, sure, I thought so too. Until she started eyeing my dad like he was the last popsicle in the desert."

Luis raised an eyebrow. "I have to say I didn't really notice that."

"How could you miss it? I swear, that bamboo bimbo better leave my dad alone."

"Amelia!" Felicia gasped.

"What's a bimbo?" Luis asked.

Amelia already regretted using the misogynistic term. "I shouldn't have called her that. Forget I said it."

"But what does it mean?"

"It's derogatory toward women," Felicia said. "Right?"

Amelia sighed. "Yes, which is why I shouldn't have said it. And what's up with your vocabulary, Luis? It's like you've lived under a rock all your life!"

"Uh." Luis shuffled his feet awkwardly. "So, are we going bowling or what?"

"Absolutely!" Felicia grabbed Amelia's arm and began towing her toward the sidewalk, one hop at a time. "Come on. Let's go."

As they walked (and bounced) toward the bowling alley, Amelia's thoughts returned to the scene at the clinic. She kept remembering how Debbie had sprung away from her dad when they walked in. Had they been hugging?

Or gah, even worse, kissing?

Bad enough if her dad was romancing someone, but for it to be Debbie—there was something seriously wrong with that woman. The bamboo plant's remains were proof of that. Amelia didn't even know how those could be explained. "Please tell me you guys noticed the bamboo."

An awkward pause followed. It was becoming a way of life for Amelia.

"Sure, we noticed the plants," Felicia said. Her voice wasn't quite as chipper as usual.

"Debbie's always liked bamboo," Luis said. "I–I mean, to grow and stuff."

"They brighten up the clinic too," Felicia said. "I think it's kind of neat she decorates your dad's clinic with her bamboo."

"Well, sure," Amelia said. "I mean, I could get bringing in a plant or two, but I swear the clinic's got a plant in every single room. And they're all bamboo. And did you see what happened to the main plant?"

"Um, which one is that?" Luis asked. "I think I counted four in the lobby."

"And that one right inside the hall leading back to the exam rooms," Felicia said.

"And the small one sitting on the counter," Luis added.

"Right. But what about the one that was sitting behind her?"

Luis and Felicia glanced at each other. Felicia shrugged and Luis admitted, "I didn't notice one there."

"Well, I did," Amelia said. "This morning, it was huge, like seriously ginormous. It reached the ceiling, guys. Anyway, it wasn't there yesterday. Yesterday, there was a different plant, wider around, but not as tall. That plant is missing today, and the one in its place… Did you guys happen to notice what it looked like this afternoon?"

"Not really." Luis looked a little worried.

"Probably because it wasn't even there."

"What do you mean?" Felicia asked.

"Well, the pot was there, the exact same pot from this morning, but the plant that reached the ceiling earlier today was completely gone. There was dirt scattered on the floor, and the soil in the pot looked all churned up, almost as if someone had yanked the bamboo out by its roots. How do you explain that?"

"You're probably just imagining things," Felicia said.

Before Amelia could protest that assumption, Luis spoke up. "Or maybe Debbie just likes moving the plants around."

"Every single day? That doesn't even make sense! And even if that were true, why was there dirt all over the floor, and why did the soil in the pot look like a tornado hit it?"

"I don't understand." Felicia bounced to a stop. "What are you suggesting, Amelia? That Debbie's destroying her own bamboo plants?" She hopped a couple times in place. "That she's what? Some kind of bamboo killer?"

Luis snorted. "Debbie Panda, the Plant Murderer."

"No, no," Felicia said. "Debbie Panda, the Bamboo Serial Killer."

Amelia rolled her eyes. When they put it like that, she did sound a little paranoid. "Fine. Forget I said anything. I'm sure Debbie's perfectly normal."

"Well," Felicia said slowly, "I wouldn't say that. I mean, she *was* ogling your dad's tail."

four

the rescues

"NOW, AMELIA, YOU know we can't keep all these animals."

"Yeah, but why not at least Squeakers? We don't have a guinea pig yet."

Debbie looked up as George and Amelia walked into the clinic. They were both carrying a couple carriers. "Are these the other rescues?"

"Some of them," George told her before turning back to Amelia. "Maybe if I thought we were the best family for Squeakers, I would consider it. But she'll never be happy with us. Not when she freaks out every time one of the cats goes near her cage."

"I could keep her in my room, close the door so the cats can't get to her."

"And how will the cats feel about that?"

Amelia sighed. "She's just so scared, Dad. I don't want to traumatize her even more by sending her off with a stranger."

"And that's why we're going to be very selective as we choose her adoptive family, okay?"

"Fine, but she has to like them, Dad."

"Of course."

"And they can't have cats."

"Absolutely."

"Who's Squeakers?" Debbie asked, tired of being ignored.

"Only the cutest little guinea pig ever," Amelia raved. "I'm going to bring her in, okay, Dad?"

"That's fine, sweetheart."

"Are you bringing all the animals here?" Debbie asked.

"I figured it'd be easier for people to visit the animals before the event if they're all in one place." He looked around the clinic. "After all, we have plenty of room."

It was true. The clinic was huge, designed to care for animals of all sizes. Still… "How many animals are we talking about here?"

"I think last count was forty-one. Or was it forty-three?"

"Are you serious? You have forty-three animals at your house?"

"No, no, of course not. Seventeen of them are already here."

"Right." Debbie felt faint. Who was going to be in charge of feeding all those animals?

"Here she is!" Amelia announced as she walked in with two small carriers in hand. "Squeakers the guinea pig." She held up one of the carriers. "And Wally the ferret." She held up the other.

Debbie's nose twitched. The ferret's scent was overpowering, completely drowning out the scents of the other animals.

"Is this all of them?" Debbie looked at the seven carriers sitting in the lobby.

George laughed. "Not even close. Amelia and I are heading back to the house for a second round. Why don't you start moving these guys in?"

"But I want to stay and get Squeakers settled," Amelia protested.

"You can help get her settled later. Right now, I need your help."

"Fine. Will you leave Squeakers for last, Debbie?"

"Sure. I'm going to get started." Debbie grabbed a couple carriers and headed back to the kennels.

An hour later, she had three cats, three rabbits, two chinchillas and a ferret settled in kennels, happily munching on some treats.

She headed back to the lobby for Squeakers and hesitated as a new scent reached her sensitive nose.

Surely not.

She hurried into the lobby and picked up Squeakers' carrier. Since all the other animals had been relocated farther into the clinic, their scents had dissipated from the lobby, allowing Debbie to truly scent the guinea pig for the first time. The poor thing was terrified, the smell of its fear almost overpowering everything else. Still, beneath guinea pig and fear, there was the faint tinge of something more.

Debbie picked up the carrier and set it on the counter, leaning forward to peer inside. "Hello, baby. Are you okay in there?"

The guinea pig scratched at the floor and squealed, the sound of her high-pitched terror making Debbie wince. "It's okay, darling. No one's going to hurt you. It's okay. Shhh. Shhh. I'm going to take you out, okay?" Debbie opened the carrier door and reached inside.

Squeakers hunched down, trying to make herself as small as possible.

Debbie scooped her up and brought her close. Cradling the terrified pig, she buried her nose in Squeakers' fur and inhaled. Fear. Pig. And . . . "Oh, no."

This was terrible.

She should call someone.

David. He'd know what to do.

Debbie grabbed the phone and had just finished dialing the number when the clinic door opened and Amelia raced inside.

"Oh good. You haven't gotten her settled yet."

"No, I was just—" Debbie wasn't even sure what she was going to say. *I thought I'd take the guinea pig home with me? I thought I'd get the mayor to adopt her?* Before she could even think of how she wanted to finish her sentence, Amelia scooped Squeakers out of Debbie's hands.

"I'll go choose her kennel," Amelia said as she walked toward the back.

"Shoots," Debbie whispered.

"Hello? Hello? Debbie is that you?"

"Oh, David." Debbie put the phone to ear. "Sorry, but we have a situation at the clinic and—"

The door banged open and George appeared, struggling with a giant kennel. "Amelia! Where'd that girl go?"

"Oh, no," Debbie muttered. "David, I have to talk to you, to the entire Council, but I have to go right now. Set it up, would you?" Without waiting for a reply, she hung up and hurried to help George.

Just as she reached him, the kennel he was shoving in the door lunged forward. Debbie sprang back. "Wh-what's in there?"

George laughed and gave the kennel one last shove, pushing it fully into the lobby. "Not sure, but I think he's a mix of German Shepherd and Siberian Husky."

Debbie leaned down and peeked inside. "Oh. He's beautiful," she whispered, cataloguing his features. Blue eyes. Huge build. Gorgeous coat of fur. Unable to resist, she opened the door and the dog instantly barreled through the opening.

He raced around the room, sniffing at all the corners before hurtling back to Debbie and George. He wrapped himself around their legs, weaving between them before darting away again.

Debbie laughed. "He's full of energy, even with only three legs."

"Yeah. I'm not sure what happened to the leg. There's evidence of an old surgery, so I'm guessing he had a family to take care of him at one time. He was skin and bones when we found him though. No tags, no microchip. We put up some signs in the area where we found him, but no one ever claimed him."

Debbie didn't understand half of what George was saying, but she did understand this beautiful dog had been homeless, with no one to care for him, when George had found him. "Poor thing."

"Yeah. Amelia loves this old boy. She named him Knight because of his gray coat. She said he looks like he's wearing a suit of armor.

Debbie smiled. She knew what a knight was, and the dog didn't look anything like one. How could he when he was 100 percent dog, not even a tiny bit of human anywhere inside him? Still, it was a charming idea.

"Oh, you met Knight." Amelia rushed into the room. "Isn't he the best dog ever?" She plopped onto the floor, and Knight raced over to her. She threw her arms around his neck and hugged him. "Yes, you're a good dog. Yes, you are."

Debbie chuckled. "How's Squeakers?"

Amelia's smile died. "She's upset, as usual. Terrified, digging at the floor of her cage, squeaking and squealing. She's breaking my heart, Dad. Can't we just take her back home?"

"Amelia, she acted the exact same way at home. The poor thing's not happy with us. You put her in her own room, right?"

"Yeah. She's in Kennel Room D."

"Well, there you go. At least in there, she won't be terrified of all the other animals, which is already an improvement from our house."

"But she's all alone, Dad! I don't want her to be lonely."

Neither did Debbie. "I bet we can get people to volunteer to guinea-pig sit. You know, so there's someone in the clinic 24-7. It's a good idea, anyway, with all these animals here."

"I've been thinking about that," George admitted. "Was wondering if maybe I should plan to move into the clinic until after the event. But I don't want to leave Amelia alone at the house."

"I could move in too, Dad! We could use the emergency waiting room. Those couches are really comfortable."

"And who's going to take care of our animals at home?"

"Well…"

"You guys don't need to worry about Squeakers," Debbie interrupted. "I'll move in here and make sure she's taken care of. Her and all the animals. It's not a big deal. I don't have any pets or kids at home, so I can move in for the duration. It's just three weeks, right?"

"Are you sure, Debbie? It's a lot to expect," George said.

"I'm sure." It would solve a lot of her problems, like getting the Town Council into the clinic when George and Amelia weren't around.

"All right, then. If you'll get Knight settled, Amelia and I will work on bringing in the rest of the animals."

"Sounds good. Come on, Knight." Debbie slapped her leg.

Knight surged to his feet and followed her to the back of the clinic.

five

a shifter rescue

"WHAT'S THIS ALL about, David?" Jessica asked.

"I honestly have no idea," David said. "I got a call from Debbie saying we have a problem and to arrange a meeting with the Council."

"What kind of problem could there possibly be?" Steve asked. "We literally just approved the event yesterday, and already there's a problem?"

"This does not bode well," Maggie said.

"Maybe the human's changed his mind," Joe suggested. "Maybe we won't have to hold the event after all."

"That's a little optimistic, especially for you, Joe," Maggie said.

"She's right," David said. "If George had changed his mind, Debbie would've been super excited when she talked to me. She wasn't exactly thrilled when I broke the news about the event."

"I'm here. Sorry I'm late. Had a bit of trouble getting away from the clinic." Debbie bustled into the room, a harried look on her face. "And by the way, no offense, but you guys totally suck."

"Hey!" Steve exclaimed.

"How is that not offensive?" Joe growled.

"It's not offensive when it's the truth! I mean seriously. Do you have any idea what it's like to work with George Finch?" Debbie waved her arms in the air. "I mean, don't get me wrong. I like the guy! He's a nice man, genuinely cares about the animals—all of them, even the ugly ones! Even the scary ones." She started to pace around the room, circling the table in long strides as she waved her arms and continued ranting, "So yeah, okay, fine. I like him. I mean, what's not to like? He's a good dad, a great vet, and super strong. I mean, like shifter-strong. The man muscled into the clinic a hundred-pound dog inside a pen I couldn't even lift when it was empty. So yeah, I like George. I don't even mind his absent-mindedness. It's actually kind of cute, once you get used to it." Debbie stopped her pacing and just stood there, staring into space, a strange look on her face.

David could tell the other council members were wondering the same thing he was. Was Debbie Panda seriously falling for their human vet? And if she was, would that be a good thing or a bad thing? David thought about that for a moment. He honestly wasn't sure.

"Uh, Debbie?" Steve said.

Debbie jerked in surprise, shook her head sharply and started to pace again. "Just because I like George doesn't change the fact that working for him is crazy challenging." She whirled and pointed her finger at the Council. "And you guys just made it worse!"

And then with long strides, she was pacing and ranting again. "Do you have any idea what I dealt with today? Do you?" She waved her arms in the air as she paced around the table. "George Finch carted into the clinic *twenty-six* animals! And we had seventeen there already. That's forty-three animals, people! Forty-three animals I'm now responsible for feeding and cleaning after and generally caring for until they all get adopted in two weeks time." She stopped pacing and faced the table. "And let me be clear." Debbie leaned forward and placed her fists on the table and slowly made eye contact with each Council Member sitting there. "If all forty-three animals are not adopted at the end of this event, I will divide the remaining animals between the lot of you and deliver them to your front porch. And if you do not properly care for them, I will report you to George. No! I will report you to Amelia. That girl will rip you to shreds. Don't think just because she's human that she doesn't have the power to eviscerate you if you harm her animals in any way."

"Is this the problem?" Jessica asked hesitantly. She glanced at David.

David didn't have a clue, so he just shrugged, unwilling to draw Debbie's attention his way. If this was the problem, though, that wasn't so bad. David had already done the math after George gave them a rundown of his rescues. He'd already figured out there'd be anywhere from thirty to fifty animals up for adoption. That wasn't so many, he thought. If every family agreed to adopt an animal, they'd actually need more rescues.

"Of course that's not the problem," Debbie shouted.

David was so startled he jumped and almost knocked over his glass of water. Cheeks burning, he righted the glass and glanced around the table. He was terribly relieved to discover he wasn't the only one startled by Debbie's fury. Steve was practically sitting in Joe's lap, so desperate was he to get away from her.

"The *problem,*" Debbie shouted, "is the *shifter* guinea pig that George Finch somehow managed to rescue"—she made air quotes around the word rescue—"and now wants to adopt out like she's some kind of pet!"

"What?" David surged to his feet. He didn't know why he was

suddenly on his feet. It just seemed the right thing to do.

"Is it a full-grown guinea pig?" Steve asked. "Maybe it's one of those shifters gone wild we're always hearing about."

"Not even close," Debbie said. "I think it's a baby."

"A baby?" Maggie looked horrified. "Who would abandon their baby?"

"Hold on a minute." Joe pulled out his phone. "Shiftoogle, help me out here." He started tapping away. A few moments later, he exclaimed, "Found it! I knew I'd read about a missing guinea pig!" He turned his phone and showed the headline from the online news agency, *Shifter Times:* "Baby Guinea Missing from Scene of Accident." Joe scanned the article. "So the parents were on their way home to Rodentville when they got caught in a freak thunderstorm and their car slid off the road. Apparently, the parents were knocked unconscious for a short time. When they woke, their baby was missing."

"I remember this," Jessica said. "But that was a while ago. Has George had her all this time?"

"No," Debbie said. "He told me all about the guinea pig he rescued just last week. He said he was in the parking lot of a hardware store in Morgan Town, heard squeaking under a bush, and there she was."

"Morgan Town," Joe said. "That's where the crash happened. There were search parties in that town for weeks, but they never found her."

"The poor baby was probably terrified," Debbie said.

"Wait. Are we seriously thinking this baby guinea pig survived all those weeks on her own before George came along?" Steve asked. "Didn't this happen a while ago?"

"Hold on." Joe scrolled up to the top of the article. "I'd say so. The article's a month old."

"The poor thing. We'd better get in touch with the family, see about getting them up here to claim their baby," Jessica said. "They'll be so happy."

"Wait," Debbie protested. "George and Amelia think they've rescued a real live guinea pig. And they're expecting to arrange an adoption for her. How do we manage that?"

"We could have the parents apply to adopt her," Maggie said.

"You don't know Amelia very well," Debbie said, "but I guarantee you, that girl is determined the guinea pig will go the right home or no home at all. What if she doesn't like the parents? And if that were my baby, no one would be giving me permission to claim my child. I'd just march into that clinic and claim her. And you know what'll happen the second they do that?"

"What?" Joe asked.

"That guinea's gonna change back into a cute little human baby, and our secret will be out."

David groaned. "What are we going to do? We can't keep that baby from its parents."

"How do we even know this is the right guinea pig?" Maggie asked.

"Do you seriously think there are two guinea babies out there, Maggie?" Debbie demanded.

"Well, no, but I just think we should be sure before we go raising those poor parents' hopes."

"That's a good point," David said. "Maybe we could take a picture of her, send it to someone in Rodentville who knows the family?"

"That won't work," Joe said.

"Why not?"

"According to the article, she was barely a year old when the accident happened and hadn't yet experienced her first shift."

"Which means no one knows what her guinea side looks like," David said.

"Exactly."

"A year is really young for a first shift," Jessica observed.

"Yes, but the trauma of the accident, her parents being unconscious." Maggie sighed.

"That poor child," Steve whispered.

"So what are we going to do?" Debbie asked. She pulled out a chair and sat at the table. "You guys made it clear my number one job was to keep George and Amelia from discovering the truth about the shifters he treats in his clinic. I can't guarantee what will happen if we don't get that guinea pig out of their custody fast."

"We could just take her. You know, break into the clinic, steal the guinea pig, take her straight to Rodentville," Joe suggested.

Debbie was already shaking her head. "No way. You're not going to traumatize George and Amelia that way. Amelia's bonded with that guinea pig. She'd be devastated and would blame herself for leaving Squeakers at the clinic."

"Squeakers?" David grinned.

Debbie rolled her eyes. "Amelia's name for her."

"If it's really the missing baby, her name's Missy," Joe said.

"Okay, next time I'm alone with her, I'll see if she responds to that name. But seriously, guys, we have to do this in a way that doesn't cause more harm than good."

"It's harmful to keep that baby away from her rightful parents," Jessica said.

"It's also harmful to give them false hope," Maggie countered.

"We need someone to come in and adopt the guinea pig," David said. "Whether it's Missy or some other shifter baby, we have to get her away from the humans and into shifter care."

"It can't be someone from Shifterville," Debbie said. "Amelia will expect to visit the guinea pig if she's adopted here. We need to get her out of town, into shifter care elsewhere."

"I'll call the mayor of Rodentville," David said. "It's really the best place for her, no matter who she is. Even if she's not Missy, there are a lot of guinea families living in Rodentville. Surely one of them would be willing to foster her until her real family is found."

"Is the mayor a guinea pig?" Debbie asked.

"No, she's a beaver. Why?"

"I just can't guarantee Squeakers won't shift if she's in the presence of another guinea pig. I'm honestly not sure what's keeping her from shifting." Debbie sighed. "I'm guessing she just doesn't know how or is too traumatized to try. I wouldn't be surprised if the moment she feels safe, she shifts. Which means the moment she truly trusts Amelia, our secret's out."

"All right," David said. "I'll call Sara, ask her to arrange for non-guinea-pig residents of Rodentville to come up here to try and convince Amelia and George to let them adopt her. We'll see how that goes." David could tell by the look on Debbie's face that she wasn't sure that plan was going to work at all, but he honestly didn't know what else to do.

"Sounds good." Debbie pushed back her chair. "I need to get back to the clinic. Apparently I'm now living there 24-7 to care for the animals."

David winced. "We'll pay you overtime, Debbie."

Debbie shook her head. "It's okay. I don't want Squeakers to be alone anyway. She's not an animal. She's a terrified shifter baby and I can't stand the idea that she's been alone since the accident." She turned away, but not before David saw the tears shining in her eyes. "Just get her adopted as fast as you can."

"Hey, Debbie," Maggie called.

"Yeah?" Debbie stopped but didn't turn back.

"It just occurred to me, if we hadn't said yes to this event, none of us would know about little Squeakers, so…" Maggie shrugged.

Debbie huffed out a laugh. "Yeah, kind of a kick in the face, isn't it?" And she hurried out the door.

six

the applicants

"CAN I HELP you?" Debbie stared at the—she sniffed discreetly—beaver shifter who stood in the doorway.

"My name's Sara." The woman strode across the lobby floor. "I'm here about the guinea pig."

Debbie nodded. "Of course." She leaned forward and whispered, "Are you the mayor of Rodentville?"

"I am. I wanted to see her, make sure she's doing okay." She cleared her throat and spoke a little louder. "I'd like to see about adopting her, if I may."

"Adopting who?" Amelia came around the corner.

Debbie bit back a groan. Amelia had pretty much been working at the clinic before and after school and on the weekends, non-stop, since the animals moved in. She did her homework here, hung out with her friends here, read her books here. It was practically impossible to get any space from Amelia, except during the days when she was at school and after clinic hours in the evenings, when she finally went home with her dad.

"This is Sara." Debbie introduced her to Amelia. "She's interested in meeting Squeakers."

"Oh." Amelia's face fell. "Okay. Well, you want to come back and see her?"

"Yes, please."

They followed Amelia to Kennel Room D.

"Wow, that's a pretty awesome cage environment," Sara said.

Debbie nodded in agreement. Amelia had set up one of their larger kennels with tunnels, caves, paper bag hideaways, and wooden blocks for the pig to chew on. None of it seemed to make a difference to Squeakers, though. As usual, she was hiding in one of the houses Amelia had set up.

"Yeah. I keep changing it, adding different things. I want her to be happy," Amelia said, "but it's not working."

Debbie's heart about broke at the look on Amelia's face. "It's okay, sweetheart. You're doing your absolute best." She put an arm around Amelia's shoulders and squeezed gently.

Amelia didn't answer. She just watched as Sara approached the kennel.

Sara was about two feet away when suddenly Squeakers exploded into terrified movement. She bolted from her house and raced around the enclosure, squealing in terror.

Amelia leapt forward, sliding in front of Sara. "You need to leave now," she said. "She's scared of you. You need to go." She turned and settled on the floor next to the kennel. "It's okay, Squeakers, it's okay," she crooned.

Squeakers froze and hunkered as low as she could to the ground, shrieking all the while.

Amelia reached in and gently pet her, crooning soft words of comfort.

Squeakers' cries slowly died away, but she continued to tremble in fear.

"Come on." Debbie put a hand on Sara's shoulder. "Let's talk outside." She led Sara back out to the lobby, where Sara staggered to a chair and collapsed, leaning forward to bury her face in her hands.

Debbie sat down across from her, positioning herself so that she could watch the hallway and see if George or Amelia appeared. "We have no idea what to do, Sara. Squeakers reacts that way to every single shifter who comes into the clinic. She acts that way with the humans too, though she's getting more relaxed around Amelia."

Sara drew in a deep breath and sat up. "Even if Amelia would approve my adoption of her, I would be afraid to take her. That was horrible. Can you imagine how fast her heart must have been pumping? I was afraid she was going to drop dead of a heart attack, just from sheer terror."

"I know. We need an applicant she won't be afraid of."

"We need to bring in her family, or at least another guinea pig shifter."

"And if she shifts?"

"I don't know. I just don't know." Sara pulled her hair in frustration. "I came with a number of prospective applicants, representing various shifter groups, just in case they were needed. I'll start sending them over one at a time. Hopefully someone will succeed where I failed."

The next several days were spent screening applicant after applicant.

Amelia was adamant that Squeakers had to like the family immediately.

Both George and Debbie tried to convince her that perhaps

Squeakers would adjust if given a little time, but Amelia insisted that time wasn't the solution. "After all," she kept saying, "Squeakers hasn't adjusted to me yet either."

And so the applicants poured in and were repeatedly rejected. None, Amelia insisted, were perfect for her little Squeakers.

Out of desperation, Debbie requested another meeting with the Town Council. "It's not working," she reported to them a week after Sara's arrival and thirty-seven applicants later.

"She's right," Sara said. "We've tried mouse shifters, rat shifters, chipmunk, squirrel and hamster shifters, gopher shifters, gerbil shifters, even lemming shifters. Nothing's working. The poor darling gets hysterical anytime they go near her. I'm beginning to think I have no choice but to bring the family to Shifterville."

"And if it isn't Missy?" Maggie asked.

Sara sighed. "I don't know, but I don't like keeping this from them. What if it *is* her? We're just traumatizing the girl and her family all the more by keeping them apart."

"Okay," David said. "But before we bring the family in, let's give Plan B a try."

"We have a Plan B?" Maggie asked.

"Yeah, I've been thinking of contingency plans all week." David sighed. "I'm thinking our best option for getting Squeakers away from Amelia and George at this point is to switch her out."

"What do you mean?" Debbie asked.

"We need a real guinea pig. I mean, a 100 percent, pure guinea pig. Then, after Amelia and George go home one night, Debbie can swap the piggies. The real Squeakers will go home with Sara to Rodentville and the newly acquired Squeakers will get adopted out, just like Amelia and George planned."

"That's pretty genius," Sara said.

"Yeah, except for one thing," Debbie said.

"What's that?" David asked.

"Amelia will notice if the guinea pig suddenly changes colors or has different markings. The girl is very observant, especially when it comes to her animals. Wherever we find this guinea pig, she'll have to look identical to Squeakers."

David nodded. "I figured. We'll get the whole town involved. There are shelters all over the place, according to George. We'll just send everyone out with pictures of Squeakers. We'll need some from all angles—top, sides, bottom. Can you get us those, Debbie?"

"Sure, but do you really think we can find one by next weekend?"

"If we get the whole town involved?" David hesitated. "Maybe."

"I'll get my people to help as well," Sara said.

"Guess we're going with plan B then," Maggie said, a worried look on her face. "But, David, what if this doesn't work?"

"We go to *my* plan," Joe said, "and pignap Squeakers."

"No," Sara said. "If it doesn't work, we call in the family and hope to manage the situation."

"And if the humans discover our secret?" Jessica asked.

Sara sighed. "Then we'll have another crisis to deal with, and this one definitely won't have a happy ending."

seven

the search

Over the following week, David spent his days listening to reports from the various residents of his town and Rodentville. A constant stream of visitors poured into his office, sharing tales of this shelter or that.

The stories were horrifying.

Animals in shelter after shelter—on something called Death Row—days, sometimes even hours away from being euthanized.

"Not again!" David stood as Sally Wolf and Max Lemur walked in the door.

Sally held in her arms a strange-looking creature. "It's a bulldog," she explained, as if David cared about any animal other than the guinea pig who was going to save their town.

"And why do you have a bulldog?" He already knew the answer, of course, because he'd already heard the answer at least seventeen times since this quest for a guinea pig began.

"They were going to euthanize him," Sally whispered, covering the dog's ears with her hands. As if he understood what she was saying. He wasn't a shifter, for the love of peahens.

"His name's Peanut," Max said.

David raised an eyebrow. That seemed a highly unlikely name.

"They told us we could change his name if we wanted," Sally said, an incredulous look on her face. "I don't understand that, do you?"

"Yeah, like we have the right to just change an animal's name without his permission." Max shook his head.

David sighed. "Yes, yes, I've heard it all before. Humans are weird, that's all there is to it. Now, what about the guinea pig?"

Sally shook her head.

"Sorry, David," Max said. "The shelter we visited told us they had seven guinea pigs, but when we got there, not one of them looked anything like Squeakers."

David groaned. "All right. Fine. Thanks, guys."

"I'd offer to keep looking, but I just can't stand it, David. All those animals. We couldn't take them all. It broke my heart to leave them behind." Sally looked as if she might burst into tears at any moment.

"I know. It's fine, Sally."

David waited until they left his office before collapsing back into his chair.

What was he going to do? There were only two days left until the event, and he was starting to doubt the viability of his plan. To make things worse, Sara had so many people involved in the search, he figured it was just a matter of time before the guinea pig's family heard about the mystery baby and showed up to determine whether she was their lost child.

He was running out of time.

A commotion at the door had him standing again.

Joe Grizzly stood there with a monkey hanging from his neck.

"What are you doing, Joe? Is that a real monkey?"

"Sure is." Joe grinned. "Her name is Lulu."

Lulu the monkey suddenly leapt from Joe's arms to the top of David's bookshelf.

David closed his eyes. "Do not tell me you adopted a monkey, Joe."

"Why not? I was at a shelter, searching for our guinea pig—no luck there—and this woman came in wanting to surrender her monkey. The shelter people told her no, and she said they were her last resort, that her next stop would be the vet to have her euthanized! So I followed the woman outside and asked why she wanted to kill the monkey, and she told me the monkey was too aggressive and wild. I mean, of course it is, David! It's a freaking wild monkey! I don't understand. So I told her I'd take the monkey."

"Do you even know how to care for a monkey, Joe?"

"Well, no, but I'm sure I can figure it out. Besides, we have monkey shifters in town. I'm sure they can give me some tips."

David groaned. "Fine, Joe, fine. But just once, I'd like someone to walk into my office to tell me they adopted a guinea pig!"

"Hey, David." Pete Rabbit stepped inside the office. "My girls and I ended up adopting a couple guinea pigs from the last shelter we went to."

Yes! Finally.

"Unfortunately," Pete continued, "they don't look anything like Squeakers."

"That's okay," David said quickly. "I know we said identical, but I'm desperate here. It should be fine as long as they're close. They're close right?"

Pete winced. "Not really. I mean Squeakers is brown and white. These piggies … well, one's black and white and the other's a solid brown. While humans aren't very observant when it comes to animals,

I'm pretty sure any human would notice how different these particular guinea pigs are from Squeakers."

David huffed in exasperation. "Who knew there were so many variations of guinea pigs in the world? I mean how hard can it be to find one brown-and-white guinea pig?"

"With a white spot on its brown nose," Joe said.

"And one brown ear and one white ear," Pete said.

David sighed. "Fine. Go on, get out of here." He turned to Joe. "And take your monkey with you."

Joe looked up. "Huh. I wonder where she went."

David froze. "Seriously? Tell me you did not lose your monkey inside my office." He bent over to check under his desk. With his luck —

Something slammed into his back with a loud screech.

David froze. Please tell him that wasn't the monkey. He slowly turned his head and looked over his shoulder.

Lulu sat on his back, a menacing grin on her face.

"Joe," David growled, terrified to move for fear the monkey might decide peacock was on the menu.

The sound of laughter was his only answer.

David slowly turned so that his back lined up with the desk, hoping the monkey would hop onto it. No such luck. The monkey just sat on his back, grinning at him.

"Joe," David growled. "Would you please remove your monkey from my back?"

The sound of Joe's chortling grew closer.

Just as Joe's shoes came into David's peripheral vision, the weight on his back disappeared.

David stood up and looked around.

The monkey was back on top of his bookshelf, grinning down at him. "Oh, for heaven's sake. Joe, please just collect your monkey and go."

"You got it," Joe laughed. "Come along, sweet girl." He reached up and scooped Lulu into his arms, murmuring, "Good job, Lulu."

As they walked out the door, Joe heard Pete ask, "Do you think I could borrow Lulu sometime? I'd love to unleash her on some of the people I work with."

David waited a moment, watching the door to see if anyone else was going to bother him. When no one appeared after several beats, he slowly settled back into his chair. Maybe he could finally get some work done.

"David." His assistant appeared in the door. "I'm sorry to keep bothering you, but George Finch is here to see you."

David closed his eyes. He didn't know why George was there, but he was pretty sure it wouldn't be to deliver good news. "Send him in."

A few moments later, George stood in front of David's desk. He was the most upset David had ever seen him, though when he thought about it, he'd never actually seen George upset. Excited or thoughtful, yes. But upset? Never.

"I don't understand what's going on, David. I've got forty-three animals ready for adoption in two days time, and I keep hearing about Shifterville families adopting cats and dogs, guinea pigs and monkeys from other shelters in other towns. I'm happy these other animals are getting homes, don't get me wrong. I'm especially happy if the animals were slated for death, but David, this is terrible. Why aren't people waiting for my event? I don't understand what's going on. Have I offended people in town somehow? We decided against the home visits."

"No, no, no, I'm sure everything's fine, George. I've heard a lot of excitement about the upcoming event. I don't think you need to worry.

There are plenty of families left in Shifterville who will be thrilled to adopt your animals. I'm sure of it."

George huffed. "Well, I hope so, David. Because if not, we'll just have to plan another event."

David blanched. He would adopt all forty-three animals himself to avoid that outcome.

eight

confession

SARA BEAVER KNEW it was time to come clean with Missy's family. She just couldn't keep this from them any longer. Especially when there was a small risk the guinea pig might actually be adopted on Saturday, by someone other than her true family.

There was no delicate way to break the news, so she just shared it. "There's a town north of here," she began. "Shifterville. Have you heard about their vet situation?"

"Is that the town with the human vet?" Carla Guinea Pig asked.

"It is. So the thing is the vet works in something called animal rescue. It basically means he helps find families for animals who are homeless. Anyway, a couple weeks ago, he apparently found a lost guinea pig in Morgan Town."

Carla gasped.

"It turns out the pig he rescued is a shifter."

Her husband, Paul, jumped to his feet. "Missy? They found our Missy?"

"We're not sure. Paul, Carla, listen. The humans don't know about shifters. They think it's a real guinea pig, and they're trying to find a family willing to adopt her."

"But she's ours," Carla burst out.

"If it's Missy, I promise we'll get her back. We're just trying to figure out a way to make it happen without revealing our secret."

"We'll go adopt her. You said the humans want to find her a family. We'll go be that family," Carla said.

"They're hosting an adoption event tomorrow, from nine to noon," Sara said. "Our main concern is that if it's Missy, she'll shift the second she sees you two. I'm not sure how to prevent the humans from witnessing something they shouldn't."

"All I care about is getting our daughter back," Paul said. "If the humans discover our secret as a result, I really don't care. We'll deal with that later. Our daughter needs us now."

"I agree," Sara said. "And if we're lucky, the residents of Shifterville will have found a non-shifter guinea pig to use as a substitute. That's the plan anyway. But I have to warn you. It may not be Missy. I don't want to mislead you. We've been unable to verify her identity. She hasn't shifted back once."

Carla turned and stared at Paul, the two of them seeming to communicate with only their eyes for a long moment.

Finally, Paul nodded.

"If it's not Missy, we'll care for her anyway," Carla said. "If Missy's truly gone forever, I'll spend my life hoping someone found her and took her in. I couldn't possibly do less for this child. If she's truly lost, we'll make sure she never feels alone again."

nine

the big day

THE DAY OF the adoption event was beautiful. The sun was shining and there was a sense of excitement in the air. It took two hours to get all the animals set up in Town Hall.

Amelia's friends had all turned out for the event, helping to set up and playing with the animals while they waited for the official start time.

Amelia worried no one would show up, but at nine a.m., when the doors opened, crowds of people surged inside. From that moment on, there was a constant stream of people eager to meet the animals.

Through the years, Amelia had worked a number of adoption events, but this one was truly unique. She'd never had so many people interested, truly interested, in the animals and in adoption. Some were interested but hadn't bonded with any of the animals there, so Amelia promised to keep them in mind for future rescues.

Poor Squeakers was terrified. Amelia kept moving the guinea pig's cage farther and farther away from the crowds, until finally it was against the wall behind two larger tables. She covered the cage with a towel, in the hopes of calming Squeakers, but kept having to lift it because so many people were interested in adopting the piggy.

Unfortunately, Squeakers shrieked in terror every time someone peeked under the towel at her. Amelia was beginning to doubt that poor Squeakers would ever have a happy home.

"I've never seen so many people interested in adopting a guinea pig before," Amelia said to Felicia.

"I know. It's pretty crazy, right?" Felicia laughed, but it sounded awkward, almost forced.

"Yeah. Crazy." Amelia rolled her eyes. "What's crazy about it is that of all those people, Squeakers isn't comfortable with a single one of them. It's like she's waiting for a specific someone, but I have no idea who that is. I want it to be me, Felicia. I want her to be happy. I just don't know how to make that happen."

"Oh, Amelia." Felicia threw her arms around her. "It's okay. We'll find Squeakers the perfect family. I promise."

"Yeah. I guess."

"I knew we should've left last night," Carla fretted.

"We still have plenty of time," Paul assured her. "We're through the worst of the traffic now, and Sara's people are keeping a watch. They won't let anything happen to our baby."

"I know. I'm just so worried. What if it isn't her? I'm so afraid we'll get there and it won't be our Missy."

"It's going to be okay." Paul kept one hand on the steering wheel and grabbed hers with the other. "No matter what we find, Carla, we won't give up. Not ever."

ten

the switch

MELVIN MOOSE WAS on a mission. For a full week he'd been searching online databases, trying to find a guinea pig to match the one Amelia's dad had rescued. Given his unruly antler situation, this truly was the only way he could help.

He couldn't go to the event itself or any of the planning sessions because to do so would mean being around girls, and in particular, around Amelia. Whenever that happened, Melvin's rack could always be counted on to make an appearance. And call him crazy, but Amelia seeing him in human form with giant moose antlers was a fairly guaranteed way of outing shifters worldwide.

Life was rather difficult for Melvin, especially at school, where he had to somehow keep his rack under control when surrounded by females of every shifter breed. On the weekends and in the evenings, he did his best to avoid females entirely. Unless he was related to them. Or his moose was intimidated by them, as was the case with the Tigers. No rack issues around them. Ever.

Worse than trying to control his rack, though, was trying to avoid Amelia. Even though they had no classes together and didn't live anywhere near each other, Melvin had lost count of the many close encounters he'd had with her, where he'd barely managed to escape before full-on rack explosion.

And so, even though he really wanted to help with the planning and execution of this event, he'd stayed away. He'd taken the path of least resistance and had avoided potential disaster in the form of his rampant rack. Finally, after a week of searching, Melvin had found the perfect guinea pig on a human website called Petfinder.

The guinea pig's name was Spot, and his markings matched Squeakers' perfectly. The only hitch was this guinea pig was male. That was okay though. Melvin figured the humans probably wouldn't even be able to tell the difference.

And so, with only a few hours to spare, Melvin and his dad were racing back to Shifterville as quickly as they could, one guinea pig named Spot in their possession.

"It's going to be close, Melvin," his dad warned. "The event's over at noon. I figure we'll get there with maybe fifteen, twenty minutes to spare."

"That's okay. As long as we get there." He peeked into his backpack where Spot was curled up, sleeping happily. "He's really kind of cute, Dad." He glanced over his shoulder at the box sitting on the backseat. "Almost as cute as them. Do you think Mom will mind that we're coming home with a few new friends?"

His dad laughed. "I'm sure she'll be furious. And then she'll take one look at them and completely melt." He grinned. "Just like we did."

They had to park several blocks away.

Once they exited the car, Carla just stood there. Terrified to take the next step.

Paul put his arm around her shoulders and pulled her close. "Come on, sweetheart. Let's go visit our girl." He lifted her chin and stared into her eyes. "Whether it's Missy or not, she's our girl now."

Carla sniffed back her tears and nodded. "I'm ready."

They walked together, hand in hand, toward the town square.

The traffic was terrible, more traffic than Melvin had ever seen in Shifterville.

They were running out of time, so he had his dad drop him off at the door. Holding the backpack with care, Melvin hurried up the steps of Town Hall. He pulled open the doors and peeked inside. There were people everywhere still. This was a disaster.

He was never going to be able to make it through that crowd without going full-on antlered out.

He searched the crowds but didn't see any of his friends. Most of the people milling around were from Shifterville, but there were some people he didn't know.

Melvin edged his way into the room and started to walk the perimeter, desperately trying to only breathe through his mouth.

His head was starting to tingle. Not good.

He squeezed his eyes shut and held his breath.

Someone grabbed his arm. "Melvin-Elvin," Paulie Porcupine exclaimed. "What are you doing here, doing here?"

Yes! Melvin opened his eyes and grabbed his best friend in a bear hug. "I am so glad to see you, Paulie. I found the guinea pig!"

"What guinea pig, guinea pig?" Paulie asked.

"The one we need to switch with Squeakers!"

"Seriously? Talk about the nick of time-time. Come on, come on!" Paulie dragged Melvin through the crowds.

The tingling was back. Melvin tried holding his breath again, but it wasn't working. There were too many people, too many of them females. He could do this. He would do this. He had to control his rack.

Envisioning his antlers shrinking to the size of nothing, Melvin shoved his moose as far deep as he could, trying to hold him back. This was going to cost him later, but as long as he managed to maintain control for at least as long as it took to switch guinea pigs, everything would be fine.

When they reached Squeakers' cage, Melvin was intensely relieved to see that Amelia was nowhere around. He pulled Spot out of his backpack and nodded to Paulie.

Paulie pulled the towel from the cage and Squeakers let out a screech of terror.

Melvin winced.

Paulie opened the cage, reached inside and pulled out Squeakers, who continued to shriek at high decibels.

Melvin quickly placed Spot in the cage and slammed the door behind him.

"Let's get out of here, out of here," Paulie muttered.

They'd only made it a couple steps when a woman ran up to them, crying, "Missy!" A tall man was right behind her. They were both crying.

From one instant to the next, Paulie went from holding a small guinea pig to a naked baby girl, who was babbling and reaching out to the woman.

The woman scooped the child into her arms and hugged her tight. The man wrapped his arms around them both and buried his face in the woman's hair. They were both sobbing hysterically.

"What's going on?"

Disaster!

Melvin had forgotten to focus on his breathing, and two things happened at once.

Amelia's scent washed over him in a wave of sensation, and the sound of her voice made his knees buckle.

The tingling in his head became a throbbing roar of sensation and he lunged around the couple and hurtled into the crowds, desperate to put space and people—lots of people—between him and Amelia.

In his haste, he tripped over his own feet and landed on his knees, just in time for both antlers to explode from his head in a massive release of pressure.

He swayed on his knees and closed his eyes, terrified he hadn't gotten far enough away. Terrified there might be more humans in the crowd than just Amelia.

Paulie and Jake were suddenly there, one on each side of him.

"Come on, Melvin-Elvin," Paulie said. "Up you go, big guy." He and Jake leaned down and helped Melvin to his feet, carefully avoiding his giant rack.

They all turned and faced the door and had taken two steps when the crowd suddenly parted, and George Finch walked right up to them, Debbie Panda at his side. The look on Debbie's face promised a world of hurt.

"Hi, boys," Dr. Finch said, flipping through some paperwork in a folder, not even glancing at them. "Glad you could make it. Amelia was wondering if we'd see you today." And he walked right on by.

Melvin swung around to stare after him and staggered from the weight of his antlers.

Jake and Paulie lunged forward and caught his arms, keeping him from becoming completely overbalanced.

Melvin stared as Dr. Finch disappeared into the crowds. "Did that just happen?"

"Um, yeah." Paulie pulled on Melvin's arm. "I think it's time, it's time for us to go, Melvin-Elvin."

"And I second that notion," Jake said. "Let's get out of here."

The boys turned toward the door and found Debbie Panda standing there, arms crossed, eyes narrowed, glaring at them.

eleven

reunion

"WHAT'S GOING ON?" Amelia asked. She leaned over and peered into Squeakers' carrier. Someone had removed her towel, but she was just standing there, staring out at Amelia, not seeming at all worried that there were strangers standing so close. Amelia's eyes narrowed. Something wasn't right.

"Are you the one who rescued our–I–I mean, the guinea pig?"

Amelia turned to face the woman speaking. She held an adorable, naked baby in her arms, and a man stood behind them, his arms wrapped around them both. "Um, no, that was my dad. I've been taking care of Squeakers though. She's a really great guinea pig, so sweet. She's been scared an awful lot." She glanced back down at the cage. "She seems fine now though. It's weird. I thought I heard her screeching earlier. I was worried, but I was busy helping a family with an adoption and couldn't get away."

"We were hoping to adopt her," the man said.

"Really?"

"Oh, yes. Can we hold her?" the woman asked.

"Um, sure. My name's Amelia."

"I'm Carla. This is my husband, Paul."

"Nice to meet you both. I'm Amelia and this is Squeakers." Amelia lifted her from the cage and turned toward them. "She's usually pretty timid and doesn't seem to like people very much, so don't be offended if—" Amelia broke off as Paul scooped Squeakers into his hands and held her up to his daughter, who squealed and clapped her hands.

"What do you think, Missy? Should we adopt a guinea pig?" Paul asked.

Missy reached out and patted her hand on Squeakers' head.

Amelia watched closely and was absolutely amazed when Squeakers let out a happy sounding squeak and nuzzled her head against the baby's hand.

Missy giggled and patted Squeakers again.

"Wow. She really seems to like you." Amelia couldn't decide which was more adorable: the naked baby with the happy squeals and kicking legs, or the squeaking guinea pig who'd just licked that baby's hand.

Missy let out a series of rolling giggles that made Amelia and her parents laugh.

Amelia couldn't help but notice both parents had tears in their eyes. "Is everything okay?"

"Oh, yes," Carla said. "Missy's been… um, sick for a while now, and, um…"

"It's just so great to hear her giggling again," Paul choked out.

Amelia nodded. It was going to break her heart to say goodbye to Squeakers, but somehow she knew, this was the right family for her. "Let's get your adoption paperwork filled out, all right?"

"That sounds great," Carla said, beaming through her tears.

twelve

the aftermath

"WELL, WE SURVIVED." David leaned back in his chair, frankly amazed they'd made it through the event without revealing the existence of shifters to either George or Amelia.

"Barely," Maggie groaned. "I'm so exhausted."

"I think we all are, but it was definitely worth it. I know George and Amelia think so. They were thrilled at how successful the event was."

"They should be," Jessica said. "There wasn't a single animal left at the end of the day. All forty-three animals adopted."

"Yeah, but some of those adoptions were just plain crazy," Steve said.

Joe let out a bark of laughter. "Did you guys see the look on Harold Mouse's face when he realized little Hannah wanted a kitten?"

Everyone laughed.

"He tried so hard to get her to go for one of the rabbits or the chinchilla," Maggie said.

"Yeah, but she wasn't having any of it," Joe said.

"Hannah knew exactly what she wanted and she played her daddy well," David said.

"Does anyone else think that Debbie might have a little bit of a crush on George?" Jessica asked.

"Hell, I noticed that all the women at the event seemed a bit too enamored of our human vet," Joe growled.

"Well can you blame them?" Maggie asked. "I mean he's just so cute."

"Right," David said, drawing the word out and rolling his eyes. How could she find the man cute? He was completely, 100 percent, boringly human!

"I'm just saying … that befuddled, distracted look really does it for me," Maggie said.

"Me too," Jessica agreed. "It's just so sexy."

David thought he might vomit.

The other men looked as disgusted as he was.

"I seriously don't get women," muttered Steve.

Joe barked out a laugh. "Good thing you don't have to then."

Steve smirked.

"Personally, I thought Amelia was going to cry when that family from Bear Town adopted those three puppies," Joe said. "She grilled that family hard, making sure they knew how to care for the pups."

Everyone laughed.

"Yeah, those bears didn't know what to do," David said.

"Things got a bit intense," Steve said. "I was actually starting to worry the dad was going to maul Amelia when Maggie vouched for them."

"Yeah, I'm still worried about that," Maggie said. "What if I was wrong? I mean, what if they looked at those pups and thought, huh, free snack."

"Oh, jeez, Mags, no one's going to eat the puppies."

"But they're bears, Steve."

A soft rumble came from Joe.

"Oh, sorry, Joe. I know all bears aren't bad, but some are crazy-mean."

"Not that family, Maggie," Joe said. "Didn't you see the little boys they had with them?"

"Boys?"

"Yeah, their triplets. They adopted a puppy for each boy. Those kids were over the moon about it."

"Well I suppose that's okay then," Maggie said.

"If you didn't think it was safe, why on earth did you vouch for them, Maggie?" Jessica asked.

"Did you see the look on that polar's face? I thought he was going to snap and transform right there, snack on the human's head or something. He was definitely tired of the questions. I figured it was the pups or the entire town."

"Jeez, Mags." David shook his head, not sure what to think about her reasoning.

"Did you guys see Debbie lecturing Melvin Moose?" Jessica asked.

Everyone groaned.

"That boy is seriously the bane of my existence," Steve said. "Do you have any idea how often he antlers out in the school hallways and classrooms? It seems every day there's at least one casualty of exploding antler syndrome. The school nurse is in the office complaining to me every single day. And the teachers!"

Joe barked out a laugh. "Karl has a new story about Melvin every week," he said, referring to his brother, the high school P.E. teacher. "He says gym class is always chaotic with so many shifter types, but that

Melvin's antlers bring it to a whole new level."

"Yeah," Steve said gloomily. "I thought for sure Melvin would have matured by now, but I swear the situation gets worse every week!"

Jessica giggled. "That boy has literally no control."

"He antlered out in the grocery store the other day," Maggie said. "I was walking to the register and suddenly an entire pyramid of canned beetles came crashing down. Of course when the dust settled, who was sitting right in the middle of all those cans? Melvin Moose, of course, antlers on gaudy display."

"Yes, well, the boy with no control saved the town today," David said.

"What do you mean?" Joe asked.

"He's the one who found Squeakers the Second and got him to the event in time. That boy managed to get into Town Hall, through the crowds to Squeakers' cage, make the big switch and almost all the way out again before he was brought down by his antlers. Frankly, when I heard about it, I was pretty impressed by his control. That room was packed with people and teen girls were everywhere."

"Wow," Steve said. "I didn't know he had it in him."

"He's one determined young man, that's for sure," David said.

"Hm, well, that being the case, I hope Debbie wasn't too hard on him," Maggie said.

"She was pretty upset at the close call, so I wouldn't count on it," David said.

"What close call?" Steve asked.

"George walked right by Melvin when he was in full antler mode, even spoke to him and everything. Debbie said it was a potential disaster of epic proportions, and the only thing that saved us was George's perpetual distraction. He apparently had his nose buried in paperwork and didn't even look at Melvin as he wandered by."

Everyone thought about that for a moment, looks of real concern on their faces.

David knew exactly what they were thinking because he was wondering the same thing.

How on earth were they going to sustain this level of secrecy and conspiracy for the rest of their lives?

It was insane and clearly the dumbest plan the Council had ever plotted.

"Speaking of Debbie," Jessica finally said, "did you guys see her sneak out the side door with that three-legged dog?"

"You mean she stole one of the animals?" Steve asked, a horrified look on his face.

"No, no. Amelia told me that Debbie was so enamored of Knight —that's the dog's name—that she refused to approve a single applicant for him. Finally, Amelia demanded that Debbie just adopt him herself, and Debbie filled out the paperwork right then and there."

David laughed.

"Sounds like there were happy endings all around," Maggie said.

"Yep, especially for Carla and Paul Guinea Pig," Joe said.

"And their daughter, Squeakers-slash-Missy," Jessica said.

David grunted, remembering his conversation with George as the man was leaving. "Yes, happy endings."

"You disagree?" Steve asked.

"Oh, no," David assured them. "It's just that everyone else's happy ending is perhaps not so happy for us."

"Why? What are you talking about?" Jessica looked worried.

"Well, George said the event was so successful, he'd like to make it an annual occurrence."

Jessica and Maggie gasped.

Steve groaned and dropped his head to the table.

Joe was the only one who looked pleased at the prospect.

David was pretty sure it was because the grizzly was hoping the next event would have a bear cub up for adoption.

Continue reading the Shifter High series at

www.ajculey.com/shifter-high.html

thank you for reading

PRICKLY TROUBLE

Please consider leaving a review on
your favorite book site.

If you would like to know when future installments
of Shifter High will be released,
please sign up for A.J.'s newsletter at
www.ajculey.com/contact.html

other books by A.J. Culey

FOR YOUNG READERS:

PICTURE BOOKS

A Fairy's Job

If My Cat Could Fly

Salsa Visits the Zoo

Taco Runs Away

TYRABBISAURUS REX

Tyrabbisaurus Rex

Revenge of the Tiger

Zombie Bunnies

FOR YOUNG ADULT AND ADULT READERS:

BENEATH THE WILLOW

Sehmah's Truth

Jennara in Flux

SHIFTER HIGH ANTHOLOGIES

Antler Trouble

Bunny Trouble

Prickly Trouble

about the author

A.J. Culey is a teacher, world traveler and writer. She lives with a number of very bossy cats and can be found at her website www.ajculey.com. She can also be followed on Facebook at www.facebook.com/ajculey.author and on Instagram and Twitter @ajculey.

T-Rab from *Tyrabbisaurus Rex* is also on Twitter @Tyrabbisaurus and can be found there when he manages to coax the laptop away from A.J.

about the illustrator

Professional cover designer and illustrator to authors and publishers worldwide, Jeanine's extensive 17 year professional background includes children's book illustration and publication, comic book art and publishing, book cover art, console game design and product branding.

She is however wondering where T-Rab took her pencils. And if in fact they still exist (she doubts it).

www.ingramcontent.com/pod-product-compliance
Lightning Source LLC
Chambersburg PA
CBHW070614310726
48982CB00001B/80
9781732328686